HOME IS A SILHOUETTE

KATARU YAHYA

SHUSH
BOOKS

Published by Shush Books
Shush Books is a division of Shaherazad Shelves
shaherazadshelves.com
Copyright © 2023 by Kataru Yahya
All rights reserved.
Our books may be purchased in bulk for promotional, educational, or business use. Please contact your local bookseller or Shaherazad Shelves or by email at publishing@shaherazadshelves.com
First edition, 2023
Cover design by Samiha Hoque
Cover art by Rose B. Gulhan
ISBN 978-1-960323-00-2 (paperback)
ISBN 978-1-960323-01-9 (ebook)

To the women who have had to turn away their faces and
scrub the shame off their bodies.
To the men who are not afraid to be human.
To you who yearn to find a home wherever. To love and
belong.
To me. To us.

CHAPTER 1
ASIYA

MY NAME IS ASIYA, and I am cursed with beauty.

People never cease to talk about my features; some say they will get cosmetic surgery done to look like me. Others look at me and then look away, intimidated. Sometimes, when my reflection stares back at me in the mirror, I wish I had never been born this way. I would prefer the type of features that are neither here nor there, not eye-catching, jaw-droppingly beautiful, nor the type that would make people only tolerate my presence. Actually, I like the latter.

Today, I wake up in darkness. I feel cold and groggy. I try to move my hands and feet but soon realize they are bound with thick ropes. I feel the concrete floor with my feet and find it damp and rough.

"Hello? Anybody there?!"

I listen for anything but hear nothing, and I begin to choke on fear. The room is so small that ten people would barely fit in like sardines in a can. There is just one window that is barred in a grid-like manner with what looks like rusted metal, and there are numerous cracks in the wall. After a while, when my eyes adjust to the dimness, I see dark red stains—which I think are blood stains—on the wall closest to me and insects crawling in crooked lines.

My head jerks upwards. I could've sworn I heard the scratching of vermin. There's no ceiling, just wood on wood and punctured roofing sheets. This feels like a bad joke, like I'm a character in a horror movie. I try to remember what happened this morning before I found myself in a grimy and gory room like this one.

I woke up particularly happy, and after praying fajr, I sauntered off to see my family. I found my mother in the kitchen, trying to put together some breakfast, while my two sisters stood around, ready to help. Our kitchen, which still smells faintly of paint—despite it being painted yellow over a year ago—is spacious. Sometimes when I'm in there, I forget I'm in a kitchen at all.

It was barely hot, kind courtesy of the large windows

barred with iron rods and the ceiling fan. We keep the kitchen squeaky clean. I mean, it's normal to keep a kitchen clean at all times, but our mother cleans the kitchen every chance she gets.

She can't stand the minutest speck of dirt, my mother. My youngest sister Zainab once commented that Mother behaves like someone with OCD in the way she repeats her strokes or rushes to swipe the counter, and on some days, I am tempted to agree with her.

I gathered from the sound of the shower running upstairs in my parents' bathroom that my father was taking his bath. I stayed in the kitchen, not wanting to risk being called lazy that early in the morning. My mother looked normal, nothing like the hysterical woman who was sprawled on the living room floor last night.

I blinked, trying to get rid of the spectacle replaying itself in my mind: Mother crying and Father ordering us to go to bed. Mother cried like someone who had lost something dear to her, like it were a matter of life and death.

When her cries quieted down, she had let loose a string of incomprehensible words—but I had heard her say a name I knew well. She always mentioned this name over and over like a ritual prayer.

Father had tried to calm her down and said he was sure Harissa was alive and well. "She has three beautiful girls now," he had said. I don't know who Harissa is, and even though I've always wondered who she is, I know better than to ask Father or Mother.

My younger sister Aisha is the boldest of us, and had asked them about Harissa the morning after we witnessed Mother's first episode, two years ago—they'd done a good job of hiding it from us until then. Father had told us in a soft tone that it was nothing to concern ourselves about and had glanced sympathetically at Mother.

Mother had simply gone pale at the direct question and remained mute the entire day. She walked like she was in a trance, and I heard her crying quietly in the kitchen when she thought we were in our rooms.

After the first few times we witnessed it, my sisters gave up staying up all through the night to discuss Harissa. The moment Father sent us to our rooms during Mother's episodes, they went straight to bed. I was the exception. I always stayed up to listen and make up scenarios about Harissa in my head.

Harissa was obviously Mother's first child, and something devastating must have happened for Mother to continue to mourn her after all these years.

I feel sorry for Mother, but I hate Harissa. She's taken Mother away from us. As much as I want some sort of respite for Mother, I hope Harissa stays wherever she is. I know, and I won't let anyone tell me otherwise, that should Harissa come back to life—or find her way to

Mother—we'll be neglected more than we've already been.

Knowing Mother, she'll spend all her time on her *precious* Harissa. We never talk about it, but my sisters and I have always felt like we're only in Mother's afterthoughts. She never neglects her responsibilities where we are concerned, so I guess she loves us too. But we don't feel her presence—like she's actually *there*.

Dr. Davis called the day after every episode and prescribed that she stay home. Father had said he was worried about her going to work after it happened, despite her protests. Her colleagues at the bank had no inkling about her condition, and he wanted to keep it that way. The doctor diagnosed Mother with PTSD after three visits and regularly refilled her medication.

We finished having our breakfast, and Father left for work at the teaching hospital. I was in the kitchen putting cups and saucers away and cleaning the kitchen with Aisha and Zainab when we heard the familiar honk of Dr. Davis's old car. Zainab rushed out of the kitchen to open the gates and let him in while Aisha and I finished up in the kitchen.

Aisha and Zainab were fond of Dr. Davis because they wanted to be doctors in the future, and he always brought them Vitamin C tablets to suck on. I went up to my parents' bedroom to inform Mother of the doctor's arrival.

The ground floor was home to the large living room, the library, the kitchen, and the store room. Mother and Father's room and offices were on the first floor, and my room was on the second floor, along with my sisters'.

The room was large and had wide windows barred with iron from behind, like the other rooms in the house. The floor was covered in beige tiles, and a heavy, lush Persian rug lay at the bottom of the bed. A portrait of Mother and Father rested above the door, and a mirrored walk-in closet stood opposite the bed. A desk sat by the window where I imagined working late into the night instead of the offices just next door from the room.

When I walked in, Mother was lying on their king-size bed, staring into space, or perhaps at the ceiling. The room was, as usual, in meticulous order, and the white sheets covering the bed were crisp and spotless.

"Mother," I said. I stayed by the door; I didn't know if I could handle seeing her cry.

She didn't flinch. She lay still, still staring at the ceiling.

"Mother," I repeated.

She turned to look at me, her big, wide eyes taking up half of her small face. She nodded and turned back to the ceiling. I took that as my cue to leave the room. I turned on my heels and shut the door quietly behind me. The quietest of noises upset her, and even though I liked to say to myself that she was fine, I didn't, for the life of me, want to upset her.

Sometimes, I want to sit with her and hold her hand. I want to talk to her about all the things a young adult without any friends feels she needs to talk about. I want to talk about school and the future and men. I want to make her feel better. I want to laugh with her and learn from her. I want to know her.

After I left Mother, I made a detour to my room to check my phone, or you could say, my best friend. My room was on the second floor of the house.

Dr. Davis's carefree laughter drifted up to my room some minutes later. I grabbed my phone and made my way back downstairs. Mother was seated in the living room by the time I got there. She wore a floral maxi dress that made her small frame look even smaller, as though she were floating in the dress, and her hair was pulled back beneath a black scarf.

Dr. Davis is a fine man. He is tall and lean, and light-skinned. His ears are quite large, and his eyes look like those of a man who barely sleeps. He always has an amused look plastered on his face, which, for young Zainab, who cannot tell it is fake, is what draws her to him in the first place. He brings a brown leather satchel with him that swings back and forth every time he visits.

Mother and Dr. Davis went through their usual

routine. He asked her how she was feeling, and she replied with a tired, "Fine." The next few minutes entailed Dr. Davis asking questions about whether *it* affected how Mother felt about herself, what she thought caused *it* to worsen, and how she was coping with *it*.

I knew *it* had to do with Harissa, but Mother's responses were barely above whispers, and we were sitting in the dining area, out of earshot. Dr. Davis finished asking his questions and gave Mother a white bottle with a blue label and cork, which she clutched in her hands.

He got up, picked his satchel from its place on the floor, and glanced our way. Zainab rushed towards him, almost knocking her chair back in the process. I got up, too, and Aisha waved, grinning before returning her attention to a video she was watching on her phone. Mother walked behind him, and I joined her to see him off. We spilled out of the living room and onto the landing.

We remained on the landing, leaning against the railing, while the doctor went down the stairs and into the compound where his car was parked. He kept it clean and devoid of dust, but the car was still old. I wondered if he would ever change his car, smiling at the thought.

I joined him in the compound to open the gates before he started the car. When he drove out, I locked up and turned to find Zainab leaning against the railings. Mother had retreated to her room.

I went back to my room, lay on my bed, and smiled at what I had planned that day: I would be visiting the museum with my fiancé and Zainab. Although I'm twenty-two and in my final year of the university—a midwifery student—Assad and I never go out alone. We're always accompanied by one of my sisters to remind us to keep things halal.

I got up soon after to pick an outfit, lifting two dresses and testing each one against my body to assess which one looked better. I'm certain people think I am self-obsessed and too aware of my beauty, but the thing is, they made me that way. If they stopped passing irritating and sometimes inappropriate comments about my looks, I wouldn't be like this.

If they didn't care so much, I wouldn't be forced to understand what a curse my beauty really is.

TODAY MARKS five years since I was brought here. And in these five years, I've learned more about surviving and serving a tyrant man than I ever could've in school. I miss school, too, but for now, I'm grateful to be alive. I've given up all hope of leaving this house; it's just impossible.

Even if I was to succeed in escaping this town, he'd find me and kill me in my sleep. I don't want that just yet. My life hasn't been what I hoped for, not that I hoped for much. There's only so little someone like me could wish or even hope to have. But I still like living. Maybe when I finally decide I'd rather die than continue simpering and bowing, I'll leave. Then I can die.

Today is also my twenty-sixth birthday. I've never cared much about my birthday or any specifics about myself. But today, at this ungodly hour while the world slumbers, I can't help but think about a parallel life. A life I would've had if Mami and Baba hadn't died.

Or plainly put, if cancer hadn't killed Mami, and if he hadn't brought me here after killing Baba for failing to pay up. I would've graduated from university by now, doing what I love the most: making things.

I've always loved art and media. Sometimes, when I'm idle, I draw in the sand at the back of the house. I draw Mami and Baba's faces—what I remember, at least.

Maybe I would've woken up to a surprise party. Mami often threw parties for the three of us at the slightest opportunity.

She had organized such parties for me since I was fourteen, and I'd had the liberty to invite five friends each time. I always invited the same two people though; Ruth and Bella from secondary school.

The three of us were friends and had lived on the same street since we could remember. Ruth's mother was a seamstress, and she lost her father to a lorry accident. They struggled to get by, and Ruth usually wore the plain clothes her mother sewed for her. It set her up to be avoided by our schoolmates.

Bella's parents were divorced. Her mother, a primary school teacher, had not conceived again after birthing her. Her father had gotten a younger woman pregnant, and when she bore him twin boys, he left her mother. Bella lived with her mother, and though she visited her father during the holidays, she despised him secretly as she did his new family.

The three of us had been the social pariahs of the school. I was from a middle-class family, like most people in school, but I was shunned because of my faith. My hijab was yanked from my head more times than I could count.

When Mami had gone to see the school's management about it, Principal Henry cleared his throat one too many times and avoided Mami's eyes as he told her it was typical school children's behavior. After he said that, he glanced at the empty sheets of paper on his desk. He made a feeble attempt to arrange them—even when they were already arranged—as he suggested that Mami move me to a school more suited for my faith if she was worried about my safety.

Mami was left speechless, but I hadn't expected any different. She rose from her seat without a word and exited the office with me following close behind. Before leaving the school, she looked at me with worry mixed in the tears that were threatening to fall from her eyes.

I held her hand with my right one and rubbed my thumb back and forth against it like she did whenever I was upset, telling her without words that I could take care of myself.

That afternoon, when I got home, she'd sat me down to

tell me that this was the way of the world. You were treated with disdain and ostracized for being different. You suffered and worked hard at being seen, but you were still a nonexistent entity in people's lives—just a speck that could be thrown away with the flick of a finger.

Those who looked at you only saw the things that made you different. Your place was in the afterthought of people and always worthy of all things demeaning. The world didn't want to hold space for people like you, but you had to live for yourselves.

Mami urged me to welcome people, no matter their differences, and to shield myself from the bitterness that was sure to attempt to consume me. I had looked at her then when she spoke, her round body and face and wisps of grey hair. Her face crumbled in despair one moment and lit up in optimism the next as she recounted her anecdotes of Islamoprejudice. I wondered how she remained kind and thoughtful when the world was nothing but a sickening place that painted rejection on our faces. Whatever we gave to the world, it spat out into our faces.

The abuse had continued and worsened. Once, when I removed my hijab in the bathroom at school to fix my scrunchie, a few girls in my class chanced upon me. They swooned at how silky and shiny and jet black my hair was and repeatedly asked me why I cover hair that every girl would kill for.

I didn't reply; I only smiled. As I turned to leave, one girl with small eyes and ears and a naturally pouted pair of lips said to her friends that I was being forced to do it. I stopped in my tracks and looked at her coldly, but that only seemed to spur her on.

She went on and on about how Muslim women are repressed and forced to do things they'd rather not do. I could listen no more—I rushed out of the bathroom, pressing my index fingers into my already filling and burning eyes.

All through my days in secondary school, I avoided meeting the disapproving gazes of people. A pastor's daughter once cornered me in an empty classroom and attempted to pray for me. She said I needed help breaking free of my false, cult-like faith. She tugged at the ends of my hijab while she sprinkled drops of anointing oil on me. I tried to cover my eyes and keep my grip on my hijab.

Sometimes, I went home with the unthinkable written on my bag and books with permanent markers. Some wrote it on my desk and in the bathroom at school, as they did with the other two Muslims in school.

"Better relocate to a Muslim country."

"There's no place for you here, in case you haven't noticed already, dummy."

"Want some pork?"

"Take that thing off your head before I yank it off and strangle you with it."

"You thought Principal Henry would take your side, huh? He hates you and your people as much as I do, stupid. He's just polite and liberal."

"You and your people don't deserve to be here."

"How does putting your head to the ground five times every day feel?"

There were times I wanted to stand up for myself—and my religion. But my lips always stayed clamped together, and the roof and floor of my mouth hugged like lovers.

I tried to the best of my ability to hide it from Mami— she had just been diagnosed with breast cancer, and I didn't want to cause her any more anguish. But sometimes, the writings would be crossed out beyond recognition by the time I woke up.

Ruth had been shunned because her family was poor. People spread rumors about her family and her father's death—he died from a stroke. Some made retching sounds whenever they were in the same place as her. The teachers were sympathetic, yet they never tried to stop it.

Bella was shunned because her family was agnostic, and her elder sister was rumored to sleep with men for money. The bit about her sister was true, but Evelyn was one of the kindest people I knew.

Bella didn't care and once beat a girl in our class to a

pulp when she mentioned her sister. The loud and blatant rumors had subsided into whisperings, and people avoided her. We occasionally wondered what it would be like to be accepted and loved, but most of the time, we drew content-edness from our proximity and shared troubles.

I wonder how they are, if they are well, and if they miss me. To them, probably, I disappeared without a trace the day my father was found dead in our living room.

I've never been a very social person. Mami and Baba's death made me retreat into myself all the more. I'm aloof all the time. On one level, that's the best thing to do around here if you want to survive.

I learned that very early on in my stay here when Femi befriended everyone in the house. He could always be seen chatting or laughing over an inside joke with another person. It proved to be his downfall.

One day, the tyrant lined us up in his occasional eerie way. He demanded that the one who sparked up a conver-sation about his dirty business own up, or he wouldn't see the light of day when he found out.

The foyer hushed like a cemetery that day. You could hear a leaf fall. Mari, whose real name nobody knew, suddenly spoke up and mentioned Femi. The poor man wished the ground would open up and swallow him whole.

Just a few days prior, I had seen him and Mari in deep conversation while picking vegetables from the garden on my way out to run an errand. He'd thought they were friends. Nobody had bothered to tell him to learn to shut up and pretend you didn't witness filth and murder around here.

The next day, the boss's cronies hauled Femi's body, wrapped in a stark white cloth, into the boot of the van. At least he was clothed with a sham of purity in death. It had been disconcerting like all the previous murders, but this was the way of the master, and we are but pieces of his mansion.

My memory of Baba's death very rudely invades my mind, and my eyes sting. I blink and ball my hands into fists. I've tried to forget, but this is the sort of thing that haunts the life out of you, especially when you're powerless and scared out of your wits.

I hate him. If I could do to him what he did to Baba, my soul would burst from sheer glee. He has ruined me. He doesn't deserve to live, but it is the terrible ones who always stay alive.

I close my eyes momentarily and see his sickening Cheshire-cat grin hovering over Baba's lifeless body like a curse. I try to hold on to the image, to feel the hate just a little while longer. To make me want more than anything to live. To await the day of his retribution. But my eyes cannot stand the torture. They open and drink in the darkness of my room.

Twenty-six years old, and all I can do is hope I don't meet the same fate as my parents. Maybe, I would've been married and started a family of my own. I've always loved children and idealized having them. I know motherhood isn't a walk in the park, but the thought of having mini people who have formed inside me fills me with nothing less than pure thrill.

This sounds far-fetched, but maybe Adam could've noticed and loved me as I did him. I'd been in love with him since our secondary school days and always secretly wished he would notice me in the shadows.

When that didn't happen, I had hoped after we graduated from secondary school that we would attend separate universities—I wanted to condition my heart to forget his existence. However, we got into the same university and my feelings for him intensified.

Ruth hadn't continued to university, so Bella and I usually went over to the cramped apartment she shared with her mother to catch up. Even with them, I was secretive. But they observed my silent interest in Adam and advised me to forget about him and learn to love someone else, even if from a distance.

I was beautiful, just a bit socially awkward, they'd said. Any guy would be lucky to love me. I wanted to heed their advice, but it was the hardest thing for me to do at the time. Whenever I was idle, I imagined Adam and me having a life and family together, but it only worsened my situation. It was like an ache that could never be pacified, and one that never wanted to go away.

My plump lips stretch into a wry smile. Those feelings are very alien to me now. They dissipated as silently and suddenly as they crept up on me. Everything has transfigured into a perpetual dullness and nothingness that wakes me up with every swelling of the sun and lulls me to sleep when darkness comes.

CHAPTER 3
ASIYA

I'M SUDDENLY VERY COLD. The silence is unnerving. I pinch the flesh of my arm so hard that the area reddens. It's not a dream. I'm terrified. I've only seen these things in TV shows. How is it happening to me? I can't even tell how much time has passed.

I started seeing my fiancé months after he pursued me, and I ignored him. Assad is five years older than me and works as an accountant at the Tesano branch of Prudential Bank.

We met when I was in my second year of university. I was only nineteen years old and had gone to the bank to pay my school fees. He followed me outside the bank to ask for my phone number, but I only looked at him blankly, smiled, and shook my head.

I then walked away as I was accustomed to doing

whenever a man approached me. But for the first time in a while, I was curious about a man. I dated once before meeting Assad, though not in the Western sense where sex or any other related activities could happen, as my idea of dating, and most Muslim women's, I might add, meant just talking and meeting with a guy to see if I could spend the rest of my life with him—and it was brief. I was in my final year in secondary school, but I had broken things off with him after I caught him kissing an obnoxious popular girl a year below us.

I was used to being hollered at, and Assad had been polite, but I expected my curiosity about the good-looking stranger to wear off. I wasn't one to like a man soon after meeting him.

More importantly, I was used to people's adoration bordering on idolizing me. Call me what you want, but it's hard to break away from being the woman every man wants and every woman wants to be. It's hard to act as though you don't feel the world revolves around you.

The very next day, I bumped into Assad at the stationery section of the mall and ducked behind a tall shelf. He looked disappointed when I snuck out of the mall —disappointed, but determined.

I wondered about him all week, even when I forced myself to soak in my favorite TV shows as a distraction. A month later, we bumped into each other at the beach. Not once, not twice. Multiple times—and trust me when I say I tried to avoid him.

I worried he was stalking me, but months after we started seeing each other, he'd tell me he was just as surprised as I was. Previously, he didn't try to talk to me, but boy, did he stare. His gaze always held something I couldn't decipher. Something so intense, it burned the back of my neck. At that point, he was a regular part of my thoughts.

When we met the following month at a friend's birthday party, I was with my cousin Halima, but I wanted him to try talking to me again. I wanted the satisfaction of knowing he was still pining for me. Petty, I know. I didn't care. But Assad didn't look like he was going to talk to me that day.

Trying to mask my disappointment, I grabbed Halima's hand and walked away right when the party ended. We had just turned the corner from the birthday celebrant's house when I heard him call my name in a low, insistent tone. My heart went berserk. I froze, glanced at Halima, and turned around.

"Asiya, can I talk to you for a moment?" he said. He sounded nervous, even though he looked cocky as hell.

I regarded him, my head in a slight tilt to the side. I was about to snub him again to make myself feel good when Halima tugged at the tip of my hijab. I sighed and nodded as Halima moved a few feet away to give us some privacy.

Generally speaking, Assad is handsome—dark and tall and lean—and has the body of someone who is a regular at the gym. He isn't, though, and it's one of the things I tease him about. He has heavy-lidded eyes, almost always partly obscured by his thick, rectangular glasses.

That day, I noticed him push his glasses up the bridge of his nose countless times, and I thought it was amusing. Even at our distance, I caught a whiff of his cologne—a sweet yet woodsy scent. He moved close enough not to have to raise his voice to speak and asked for my number. I gave it to him while a part of me screamed at myself for being too soft with this guy.

"What do you say about having a cup of coffee together? Tomorrow?" he asked, his question invading my thoughts of him.

"I...I...uhm," I stammered. I'm not someone who fumbles with words, even in the most dicey situations. But this man made me feel like a stammerer, even if only for a moment.

I didn't know what to say; he was the first man to ask me out to a café. And I loved cafés. I wondered if he figured it out from all the times we encountered each other.

But I liked the ego rub. All the other men who had

asked me out prior to meeting Assad tried too hard to impress me. They suggested that we go to expensive and sophisticated restaurants. And at night.

I only went out at night with my one-time girl friends and family. Yes, even at twenty-two.

I didn't have a problem with expensive restaurants, but all those men made their intentions pretty obvious. I'm not the most pious person alive, but sex is just off my radar. I'm keeping it halal until I get married to the love of my life. Allah tells us in the Qur'an to keep our horny thoughts and urges locked up, and I'm doing just that.

The first time, it was a middle-aged man who looked like he could get people to do his bidding. Well-dressed with a dark aura, I could imagine him imprisoning some-one's father just to get something out of you. I had cringed inwardly and turned down his offer politely. He had looked displeased, like he wasn't used to being rejected, but walked away without a fuss, his face grim.

The second time, I simply kept a poker face, shook my head, and walked away. The man hollered and whistled and shouted obscenities that I was only a beautiful face for men to enjoy. People kept looking from me to him, some laughing at the spectacle. My face was hot from embarrass-ment, recalling the incident.

"Asiya, are you okay?" Assad broke into my thoughts again.

"Huh? What? Oh," I said in a breath, realizing I probably had a frown plastered on my face. I still hadn't given him an answer.

He looked at me with his eyebrows raised in perfect arches.

"Yes, sure," I replied. "I'd love to."

"Great! I'll call you. Or text you. Whatever you prefer."

"Any is fine," I said, waving his eagerness away. I was ready to leave. I didn't like how this guy was melting my icy self without even trying. I nodded and smiled a little before turning to leave. I caught up with Halima and walked ahead of her. I wasn't going to let her see that I was interested in the guy.

"So?" she probed.

"So nothing," I deadpanned. That was rude, but Halima wasn't perturbed in the least.

"Say something."

"What?"

"You just got yourself a man, that's what." She giggled. I ignored her, and she didn't mention him again.

The next day began a series of coffee dates, and our relationship became official to our families after about four months. It's been a year and a half since we started dating, and I wish I hadn't been such a bitch when we first met.

That fateful morning, I had put on a pair of baggy

jeans, a black t-shirt with no inscription, a pair of brown sandals, and a black hijab. I looked at myself in the mirror and glossed my lips. After rummaging in my jewelry box, I got out my favorite pair of hoop earrings and spritzed on some perfume—Assad said he always loved the vanilla smell of my perfume.

Satisfied, I picked up my phone and purse and returned to the living room. I sprawled on the sofa, watching a show on TV while I waited for Assad to pick me up.

He was to meet me at my house at nine in the morning, but he was thirty minutes late. That was unlike him. I reckoned he had been caught up in something—traffic probably, since I know the traffic in Tesano on Mondays can get insane—so I decided to keep waiting. I couldn't blame him.

An hour passed, and there was still no sign of him; neither was there a call or text from him to explain his uncharacteristic lateness. I called and texted him, but I got no response. I was beginning to worry. I often stood at the windows, hoping to see his car coming up the dusty road.

There was still no sign of him after two hours, and just when I was about to give up and head to my room, I heard a car horn blare outside in front of our gate. It didn't sound like Assad's.

Wondering who could be calling on my parents at that hour, I left my phone on the couch and made my way to the door. I walked out of the living room and onto the landing, descended the stairs, and headed into the compound.

I opened the massive black gates only to find three muscular men wearing ski masks and leaning on a black convertible. My heart caught in my throat, and I opened my mouth to scream, but I turned mute. Before I could run back into the safety of the house, strong arms grabbed me. That is the last thing I remember before waking up in this room that gives me the creeps.

My insides twist and growl, and I wince at the discomfort I feel. I look up and out the room's single window to see that it is nightfall and, as if on cue, more pangs of hunger gnaw at my guts.

I look at the door at the sound of shuffling feet and male voices. The part of the floor under the door is illuminated by what looks like a flashlight. As the voices get closer, the smell of marijuana wafts into my nostrils, and I wrinkle my nose. The door opens, and two unfamiliar faces walk in, smirking and lighting the room with their flashlights.

One of the men is tall and lean, and the other is short and stocky. The tall one has a cigarette in his mouth, and the room is fast being engulfed in smoke. His dark and cracked lips stretch into a menacing grin, revealing filthy teeth, and I shudder. The short one directs the flashlight to my face, and my eyes squeeze shut. He holds it there for a moment, then directs it to the floor and speaks up.

"I see you are awake, missy. The boss can't wait to see you."

The tall one sniggers and adds, "And have you."

They guffaw, edging closer as I inch backward.

"You are a beauty," the short one says. "We would have you ourselves if we could. I bet you taste and feel beautiful, too." Lamps in his reddened eyes come alive when he licks his lips.

The lust on their faces forces my neck to turn to the side, my eyes squeezing shut again, so I don't come face-to-face with the blood-stained wall. I steel myself, denying them the satisfaction of seeing my eyes well up, but it is all I can do.

CHAPTER 4

LILA

I SIT at the edge of my bed, and after a while of thinking about nothing, I heave myself up from the mattress. It's finally nightfall. I had been waiting to do this like I do every day to finish my chores and retreat to my cave.

I stretch my arms and legs, exhaustion weighing on them. I walk out of my room and down the brightly lit corridor of the girls' quarters. Like the boys' quarters, there are a total of twenty-three doors, eleven on the left and twelve on the right—the twelfth one being the bathroom.

There are twenty-two of us women, and my room is the first on the left. Each door is wooden, heavy, painted, and has a knob with a lock that isn't easy to pick. We all have keys to our rooms, and so does the boss. On the last day of every month, he conducts inspections while we carry out our duties.

We are expected to keep two suitcases—at most—to hold our clothes, toiletries, and anything else that is essential. If anything is amiss in anyone's room, the person is questioned, tortured, and then murdered like Femi.

Once during his thorough, scheduled scrutiny, a sharp kitchen knife was found under Bertha's mattress. She was summoned from the kitchen, where she was washing utensils, and questioned on the spot. The men who were with the boss at the moment recounted the incident over and over until everyone knew the littlest details that happened by heart. They said the color drained from her flaky face, and her skinny hand had flown to her mouth as if trying to keep any words that she had from falling out.

She had trembled like a withered leaf in harmattan when she was being led away after remaining silent all through the interrogation. That night, we heard her screams. We didn't see Bertha again, and her room was cleared of her personal belongings in the days that followed.

The following week, a new girl was brought to the house and given the key to Bertha's room. The new girl always looked over her shoulder and jumped at the slightest thing. Nobody told her what happened to the previous occupant of her room, but I didn't think anyone needed to.

I stop at the twelfth door and push it open. I enter and

perform wudhu, taking my time to feel the biting coldness of the water as it rinses the skin of my face, arms, and feet. Then, I walk back to my room. I shift the table, which holds my small mirror and the chair in front of it, making space for the long fabric I use as my prayer mat. It feels heavy in my hand.

I finish praying and remain seated on the mat. It has been a while since I prayed. Mami and Baba loved Allah and had raised me to grow to love Him, too, never once imposing anything on me. Mami told me to practice because I want to and believe, not because of them.

While I did just that, after their deaths—Mami first, and then Baba—I became less and less practicing. I just couldn't bring myself to pray and fast like I did when they were alive—I felt like God had deserted me. Why else would all those terrible things happen to me? To people as good as Mami and Baba? And what do you do when you are angry at God for how things happen? You don't pray as much. When I do pray, it's to feel a connection to my parents.

I wish I'd never changed, though, because the numbness inside me is eating me up. And it has been growing since I stopped seeing prayer as a way to reconnect with my faith.

I close my eyes and smile when I see Baba, Mami, and myself seated at the dining table as we laugh at one of

Baba's stories. I open my eyes. I push myself up from the floor and put the mat away, hoping I pray more in the future.

Sitting at the edge of my mattress once more, I look around my room as if expecting to find something.

My room is small and painted white. Sometimes, when I'm lying on my mattress, I feel I can touch the ceiling. The room has only a thick mattress, a table and chair, and a mirror. And, of course, an old duffel bag I found in the store room which holds my belongings.

I lay on the mattress in the fetal position, shifting to face the wall. My weary eyes close of their own accord, and the day's happenings replay in my mind. The boss seemed unusually excited about something. Or someone. He ended a phone call during which he kept mentioning *her*. I wondered if he was considering getting himself a wife because he has never shown interest in women. Not that I know of, anyway.

The only women here are the servants. Who knows whom the boss sees or sleeps with outside the house? The day he shot Baba, I had expected him to have his way with me, but he never did. I had the same expectations when I learned about the girls in the basement, but he has never touched them, either. To be honest, it feels out of the ordinary to imagine that he has sex for the cheap thrill of it.

Does a beast of a man like him wait for love like the rest of us?

I tell myself I don't care, but a part of me wonders at this *her* and if she knows what she's getting herself into. Three servants cleaned one of the large and lavish bedrooms last week, and I heard them discussing the clothes and shoes arranged in the closet by color. This *her* is, by every indication, a special one.

THEY UNBIND my feet and hands. As I try to kick and bite them, the tall one hefts me effortlessly and flings me over his shoulder. He walks towards the door in long strides, his short companion close on his heels. I eventually give up struggling and close my eyes, trying to fight back tears.

His left shoulder blade bores into my skin, and the smell of his unkempt hair makes me gulp for air. They dump me in the rear seat of a pick-up and lock the doors, seating themselves in front. They speed off in the direction of nowhere. I fall asleep soon after trying to listen in on their conversations and realizing they only speak about football and women.

After I sleep for a few hours, they wake me up and drag me out of the car. I look around and see, in front of me, a mansion. It's white and looks isolated with high walls. The compound is three times the size of our compound back home, and it is laden with three vans and more than a dozen luxurious cars, each parked beside the other. There is a lot of lighting in the compound, so many that it feels unnecessary and too dramatic. Also, I can't seem to figure out the source of the lights.

Tall trees line the periphery of the compound, and I catch a glimpse of a garden in the far-left corner. The house, which looks like three different houses in one, is about seven floors high. It looms a few feet from where I stand as though beckoning me to it, but I take a step back. I look behind me and notice how far the gates are.

My captors nudge me forward, and each holds my hand, dragging me up the stairs. The mahogany doors swing open, and there he is, standing at the bottom of the staircase. I shield my eyes with my hand from the intense light from the fancy chandelier up on the ceiling. When I get used to the light, I remove my hand. This room looks like an assembly hall of sorts—the kind used for parties— and the gold-plated spiral staircase catches my eye. Wow.

He smiles, spinning the ring on his middle finger. I immediately have the urge to retch. His powdered face, expensive kaftan, gold jewelry, and overpowering perfume make me so dizzy that my lean captor has to keep me steady with his arm. His grin doesn't falter. Instead, it grows wider as his eyes go from looking right into mine to sweeping with overt lust across my body.

Mr. Debayo is the last person I expected to see. A year ago, he was one of Father's acquaintances, and after a couple of visits to our house, he told my dad of his intent to marry me. It did not occur to me at the time that this was Debayo's second time asking as one of many I had rejected as a teen.

Father politely turned down his proposal just as I had, this time adding on the fact that I am now engaged. Debayo didn't take either rejection to heart and went on in vain to convince my dad he would like to shower me with gifts on my wedding day—that he only wanted my happiness. Yet, here he is, a man of fifty, doing what I never imagined him doing.

I am beautiful; some even say I am extraordinarily beautiful. Ever since I can remember, I have had offers from agencies to be the poster girl for their products—offers I have always turned down. Debayo is just one of the many men who have declared their love and intention to make me their wife.

Now here I am, paying the price for being pleasing to the eyes.

"Welcome to your new home, Asiya," Debayo says, and it sends chills throughout my body.

"This isn't my home," I find myself saying. "My home

is with my family, and they will find me and get me out of here."

"Ah, you've found your voice. You see, we are far from Greater Accra, and soon, your family will quit looking for you. We would have married and consummated our marriage by then, I assure you, my dear. As for your fiancé, he is being taken care of as we speak. Pity you won't be around to mourn him. But never mind, you can do that right here." His eyes shine with unadulterated evil as he speaks, and my skin begins to crawl.

Before I think twice, I break free and make for the door, running as fast as my legs can carry me. I stop short when I get to the door—two tall, bald, and muscled men in shades have materialized at the entrance. Each grips my hand and drags a crying me back to where Debayo stands. He taps his right foot on the floor like an animal getting ready to pounce on his prey.

I am, in fact, his prey. An impassive expression has replaced his grin, and his eyes have turned ice-cold. As wetness snakes down my face and stings my eyes, he takes my chin between his thumb and forefinger, forcing me to look into his gaze. It looks dead. Cursed.

"Make so much as an attempt to escape, and you will not be around to bury your family." He waits for his words to elicit the desired reaction, and his grin returns when my eyes grow wider and my lips quiver.

My gaze slides to the few people I am just noticing. They are standing a few feet away from him, each with their hands clasped in front of them. They look away, except for a young woman who holds my gaze, her eyes sympathetic.

"You may not be alive to tell the tale, too," he adds. "Take her to her room."

The sun streams through the draped windows, and my eyes flutter open. I turn away from the window and lie facing the door. My eyes feel heavy. I suppose that happens after a night of crying oneself to sleep. I yawn and sit up, taking in the room for the first time.

It's twice the size of my room back home. The bed feels soft and cushiony with four pillows and stark white bedding, the type that makes you want to lie down all day. The drapery is gold-colored, and my eyes are drawn to the big-screen television that faces me. My gaze then shifts to the walk-in closet, complete with a mirror near a door that I assume is the bathroom. There are even cream-colored sofas by the door, opposite the TV.

I pull myself out of bed and walk towards the bathroom, stopping momentarily at the closet. My face is blotchy, and my eyes are puffy. I wince and continue to the marble-floored bathroom to perform wudhu and pray fajr. Fajr was about forty minutes ago, with the sun rising, but I couldn't bring myself to open my eyes earlier and face my fate.

Once I'm done, I sprawl on the prayer mat and bawl, remembering that I may never see my family again. The despicable man's threats regarding Assad fill me with foreboding doom—because now I don't think they are just threats.

I remain on the prayer mat for a while before clambering up to take a shower. I cry again in the shower, allowing the water to mix with my tears. I wear a fresh pair of baggy trousers and a shirt I find in the closet and then return to bed, burying my face in the pillow in hopes that I fall asleep again.

Just as I'm drifting off to sleep, I hear a soft knock on the door. I hold my breath and keep my alert gaze on the door. The person behind the door knocks again. I exhale and abandon the bed, precision and fear in my every step. I grip the door handle and yank it open.

I find the woman who looked like she shared my pain last night standing at the entrance, her arms hanging by her sides. The woman who never looked away. Seeing her now unnerves me a bit, and I regard her without saying a word. She has a poker face and it feels like we're in a silent staring competition. I roll my eyes, prepared to slam the door in her face and resume hiding among the bedding.

"Good morning, ma'am. My name is Lila. I'm your help."

I almost jump when she speaks. Her voice is low, and she drawls out her words one by one. I say nothing. I only nod and continue staring at her. She breaks the stare and brushes imaginary specks off her white apron.

"I'll bring your breakfast now. What'll you have?"

"Hot chocolate would do," I say while I try to smooth my unruly hair to put it beneath my scarf.

She nods and turns on her heels. I'm rooted at the spot. Something about her unsettles me. Maybe it's the faraway look in her eyes or her prim and proper demeanor. Maybe it's the way of the help, but I wouldn't know. I've never had one.

Mother always thought of hiring help as unnecessary. It's unnatural to think of a man like Debayo having no servants, though. I shut the door and return to bed, my family infiltrating my thoughts for the millionth time that morning.

I wonder how Mother is coping with my disappearance. My face pinches with worry. It's bad enough already with Harissa gone. Regardless of my feelings towards her, this could drive Mother mad.

I can't cry anymore. My eyes have decided to defy me.

Instead, my innards knock against my chest, and the dull, growing pain spreads to my entire body. I feel incapable of moving. I sigh repeatedly. I never thought I'd ever be suicidal, but right now, I'd rather be dead than alive through this nightmare.

Two soft, successive knocks bring me out of my dark reverie. I yell for the person to come in. The room echoes my now unrecognizable raspy voice, and I sink lower into the bed. The tray enters first, followed by Lila's thick body. Her eyes avoid mine as she places the tray at the foot of the bed.

I glance at the cup of hot chocolate and two slices of bread and decide I don't want to eat. She moves to close the door and stands by it. I motion for her to sit, and she does, all the while avoiding my gaze. She can feel my eyes on her. Watching. Assessing.

She sits on one of the sofas positioned in front of the television. Her eyes do not leave her worn shoes. Her arms and legs are bare, as she is only wearing a short-sleeved dress that stops right below her knees. Her legs look strong. My eyes linger on her full bosom and hips. Her face is plain, with rounded cheeks and a pair of lips set in a straight line. My eyes travel to her head. It's covered with a black netted cap, and I wonder if she's Muslim.

After two bites of a slice of bread and a few sips of hot chocolate, I push the tray back to the foot of the bed. I sit cross-legged, watching Lila as she pushes herself up from the couch and picks up the tray in three long strides. Before leaving, she glances at the food and back at me, her face spelling disapproval. I look away at the drapes. Who cares what she thinks?

HE HAS ASKED me to watch her. He said he assigned me to her for a reason. And if I don't make him happy, he'll be elated to make sure I join Mami and Baba wherever they are. Tears had knocked at the back of my eyes when he mentioned them like their deaths were his greatest pleasure.

But I gritted my teeth, refusing to allow them to pour. My refusal caused my eyes to feel like furnaces and my mind to call on thoughts that didn't belong in it.

Last night, when she arrived, we were summoned. Tiwa from the next room had banged on my door, rousing me from my dreamless sleep. I didn't get angry—nobody kept the boss waiting.

In fact, I was grateful to her. I rushed downstairs in my

nightgown and nightcap to cover my hair and took my place beside my sleepy and disgruntled colleagues. I didn't know, then, why we were summoned.

The boss stood at the foot of the staircase, a small smile playing at the corners of his lips. He looked over at the vast doors when the engine of a car died out in the compound, his pudgy hands rubbing together.

And then, they brought her in. Her eyes seemed to want to hop out of her beautiful face. She attempted to fight him. I wish someone would tell her nobody defied him. Our eyes met when everyone else looked away. Her face was tear-stricken, and her eyes had implored me for help.

I couldn't look away, even though I knew I should. I couldn't. Something in her eyes started melting the iciness I was shrouded in. I wanted to talk to her and wipe her tears. To be her friend. It was sickening to watch him incite fear in a woman that young, but it was unwise to express my displeasure in any way.

This morning, I stood at her door for a long time, my hand raised mid-knock. I didn't know how to talk to her. I had talked to just four people in my previous life, and I've stayed out of everyone's way since I came here.

My throat was suddenly parched. After talking myself into doing what I knew would please him, I swallowed and licked my dry lips, then rapped at the door. The moment the door flew open, and she appeared, her left hip jutting out and holding the door ajar, I turned mute.

My thoughts and words deserted me, and my parched throat announced itself again. We stared into each other's eyes for too long, and I could've sworn I saw her roll her eyes at one point. She still looked like she could break down and cry any minute, but her haughtiness masked it.

I opened my mouth, and words tumbled out, identifying myself as her help. She gave me a dismissive nod and raised her eyebrows, waiting for me to finish my monologue. I asked her if I could bring her breakfast up to her room, and she nodded her consent.

After I brought her a meal, she indicated that she wanted me to stay. I sat on a couch for the first time since I arrived here. I perched at the edge and waited for her to finish eating. She stopped chewing soon after she started, and fear seized me.

I turned to find her sitting with her elbows resting on her crossed legs. The tray was back where I placed it at the foot of the bed. My face was scrunched up as I picked up the tray and glanced at her.

She's going to get me into trouble if I'm not careful.

I sit on my mattress, making a huge dent in it. It went the same way for lunch and supper. She isn't eating. If this continues, my blood will be one of the many the monster has spilled. Poor girl, I can't blame her. I wonder if I should speak to her about what's at stake. I soon fall asleep, the last of my thoughts filled with Asiya and the boss's peculiar interest in her.

CHAPTER 7

WHEN ASSAD HONKED on arrival at the house, it looked like nobody was home. He tooted louder, and he heard the front door open. Asiya wasn't answering her phone. She was certainly angry, as she had every right to be, about his tardy arrival. He could explain, though. He hoped she would show some grace when he narrated the troubles he had encountered on his way to pick her up.

He lived at one end of Tesano, and Asiya lived at the other. Before their relationship, it seemed like all they had done was see each other, but if you asked them now, they would tell you, lips moving in tandem, that the distance between them was like the ocean and desert separating two countries. Then, they would look into each other's eyes and stretch their lips in matching impish smiles.

When he got to one junction, the traffic had caused the

two-way street to be awash with the deafening honking of car horns and hawkers shouting for their voices to be heard above the din. As if that wasn't exasperating enough, drivers chortled and hurled insults at each other.

It was sweltering hot, but nobody complained. The Ghanaian sun punished everyone with heat during this time of the year. The armpits of his blue polo t-shirt darkened with perspiration. The air conditioner in the car seemed to have stopped working. Assad contemplated parking his car and walking the rest of the way.

Eventually, he cleaned the sweat snaking down his face with a handkerchief and fanned himself with a book. After two hours, the traffic became bearable, and he inched his car in the direction of his lover's house.

The honking of cars didn't subside—the road was too narrow to be a double road—and drivers gave each other a hard time for it. Shops and shacks, which served as homes, sprawled on either side of the road, spreading into small settlements.

The hawkers shoved bread, chocolate, and fruits in the window, offering reduced prices. He looked straight ahead and briefly turned to smile, declining with a shake of his head.

Assad soon left the busyness of the junction, and the remaining part of Tesano opened itself up to him. He negotiated a curve and turned into the untarred road two miles from Asiya's home, leaving a puff of dust in his wake. Many houses and a few shops dotted the opposite sides of the road; each house had in front of it a tree sprouting up from the ground, with a film of dust coating its green leaves.

He recognized a black Hyundai when he took the turn that ushered him onto Asiya's street. It had been trailing him since the previous junction. The two occupants of the car wore dark suits and shades. He observed that they did well to keep their faces hidden. Alarm crept up his back and circled his neck.

His steady grip on the steering wheel grew sweaty and slippery. He passed Asiya's house and drove on until he saw the small welcome billboard signaling his arrival in North Kaneshie. He was no stranger to the town, having attended several finance workshops in the heart of the town.

He stopped at a Chinese restaurant he had frequented in the short while he stayed there. He parked and walked in, seating himself at the window. He watched them watch him, then drive away in the opposite direction. For good measure, he waited for an hour before driving off. He remained on the lookout for the Hyundai and anything that gave him the creeps. He would've texted Asiya, but he was on such high alert and did not want to alarm her before he was safe.

When he got to his lover's house, he heaved a sigh of relief and wiped the beads of sweat on his face. He slid his glasses up to where his nose met his forehead and chuckled when he felt it slide down the bridge of his nose again. He got out of the car when Zainab opened the gate a crack and peered through.

She opened it wider when she saw him, and he stepped into the compound. Zainab looked confused, as if his presence needed some explanation.

He ignored her look and strode in, making a beeline for the living room while Zainab remained at the gate in puzzlement.

"Assad?"

He heard the question in her voice and turned, slowing his pace. She didn't wait for him to speak.

"What are you doing here? I thought you had already left with Asiya."

Now, he was just as bewildered as she was.

"No. I just arrived to pick her up. I'm awfully late; I know she'll be pissed." His mouth opened, and let out a nervous laugh when Zainab remained silent. She looked like she had seen a ghost, eyes wide and jaws slack.

"But...but she's not here," she said.

"Who?"

"Asiya."

"Where did she go?"

"I...I don't know. Maybe an hour ago, Aisha and I heard the tooting of a car horn outside and assumed you were there. Then...then we heard the gates opening. We thought you two had left already. Without me."

He could hear her, but her words swirled around in his head and made his legs weak. The ground seemed to move in a circle when he looked down. He staggered forward and up the stairs to the landing and gripped the railing.

His mind went to the car, and dread poked at him from all angles. The door to the living room swung open. Aisha and their mother, Ameera, looked from Assad to Zainab, who now stood close to Assad, and back at him again.

"What's going on?" Ameera croaked. She could barely get the words out of her mouth without them trailing off.

"Asiya is gone," Zainab and Assad said together.

CHAPTER 8

IT WAS NEARLY noon when Ameera sat up in her bed, feeling her stomach folding into itself. Her thoughts and memories were an all-consuming fire, enveloping her flesh by flesh. She climbed out of the bed she shared with Harif and headed to the kitchen. Cooking always cleared her head.

Zainab and Aisha joined her shortly as she placed a saucepan with oil on the fire. She adjusted the knob until the fire was just right. She perched herself on a long wooden stool and stared into the flames.

Harissa's face materialized in the reds and blues of the fire, and Ameera looked away. Even now, she remembered her daughter's face like it was just yesterday when Madam Jean had pulled the lithe body out of her. She had been a pink little thing.

Her focus shifted to her two daughters. She had them and Asiya, but the ghosts of her past still had a hold on her. She wanted to yield to the ghosts of her past, if only it meant her seeing Harissa once more. Feeling guilty, she smiled at her girls. Asiya was out on her date, she mused. She didn't understand why the girl had left her phone in the living room. She was inseparable from that thing.

She got up to pour chopped onions and tomatoes into the hot oil. The toot of a car horn drew their eyes to the door of the kitchen.

"I'll get it!" Zainab yelled.

"You really don't have to yell, you know," Aisha said. She rolled her eyes and gave her sister a playful shove.

Ameera gave Aisha a reproachful look. "Be nice," she said before going back to her cooking. The onions and tomatoes had caramelized now. She added a spoonful of tomato paste and stirred, wondering who was at the gate. She added some chili, mackerel, and fried beef from their packaging and then stirred again.

"What's taking your sister so long?" She glanced at Aisha and adjusted the regulator so that the red and blue embers were scant. "Let's go check on her," she added before her daughter could say anything. Aisha only nodded. Ameera wiped her hands with a checkered napkin and then held her hand out for her to take.

On their way out of the kitchen and towards the main

door, the mother and daughter nursed private thoughts of how it had been a lifetime since they had body contact like this. It felt...strange to hold each other.

When Aisha pushed the door open, they were greeted by Zainab and Assad in mid-conversation, looking disoriented. Ameera and Aisha stood in the doorway. Zainab craned her neck, looking into Assad's face as if it held something she sought.

When they both said, "Asiya is gone," Ameera let Aisha's hand go and pursed her lips in confusion.

"Eh? Gone where?" She looked from Assad's face to Zainab's. She shifted from foot to foot, her frustration becoming more evident when both hesitated to explain.

"Zainab told me that Asiya isn't here and that she thought I had come to pick her up already. But I am late for our date, as something bizarre happened on my way here. I haven't seen her." Assad paused to take a breath. "Zainab said she heard a car honk and the gates open an hour ago."

"I heard it too, so where is she? Where's my daughter?" Ameera's voice was an octave higher and bordering on hysterical. Her eyes looked wider and wild as she peered into their faces, looking for reassurance about Asiya.

"I'm trying to figure that out, Ma. I thought we would call—" Assad started.

"Her phone is lying on one of the sofas," she cut him

off, gesturing with a nod of her head toward the room and gripping Aisha's hand for support.

Aisha could only look on, her mouth dry and her heart trying to take leave of her chest. Asiya leaving her phone behind only meant that there was a storm brewing.

Ameera's face had already gone wet, and drops of salty tears entered her mouth whenever she parted her lips to say something. There were no more words on her tongue. She clutched Aisha's hand again, turned, and recoiled to the room at a plodding pace. Zainab and Assad followed suit.

Aisha called her father six times and got no answer. On the seventh try, Harif answered.

"Dad—"

"Aisha? You know I'm at work."

"We need you...." Her voice trailed off. She wet her lips.

Harif turned away from the patient he had just attended to.

"Aisha, what's the matter?"

The patient looked on as shadows crossed Dr. Harif's face. She stood up, awkwardly shoving her purse under her armpit and clutching a sheaf of requests and prescription forms.

She limped towards the door, the left side of her body carrying her weight. She pretended to have trouble with the lock long enough to keep her ears in the room. She scrambled out when the nurse shot her a hard look.

"It's Asiya!" Aisha dropped the phone and covered her face with her hands, her body shaking with each sob.

Harif called Aisha's name repeatedly, but all he could hear was muffled crying. He explained to the attending nurse that there was an emergency at home and grabbed his briefcase, making for the door.

The patients waiting to see him watched in confusion as he sped past them toward the parking lot. The nurse came out after a brief moment to announce that their appointments would need to be rescheduled. Almost every one of them looked disappointed.

Some masked it, while others wanted the world to sense their displeasure. They glared at the space where Dr. Harif had walked, mouthing words and dragging their feet. The nurse sighed and turned to leave. Patients could never be reasoned with.

Harif's chest squeezed as he waited to be let in the house. Assad opened the gates while avoiding the older man's eyes. Harif had not an inkling about what was happening, but his gut wound and unwound all the way to the living room.

Assad's silence and demeanor as he followed him into the room made him wonder. He met a subdued atmosphere. His wife was seated on the linoleum floor, her fist supporting her cheek. When she lifted her head, his hand flew to his mouth.

Her eyes were bloodshot and swollen, and her face was smaller and pained. Aisha and Zainab held each other, white lines crawling from the corners of their eyes down to their chins. Assad looked no better as he lowered himself onto a couch, his glasses lying beside him. Asiya was absent. Harif dropped his suitcase and rushed forward, unsure who to go to.

It made sense to go to his wife first, so he did. He knelt beside her, taking her free hand in his.

"What's going on? Where's Asiya?" He turned his neck this way and that, hoping his eldest daughter would pop up out of a cloud of smoke.

Silence.

"Assad?"

Assad dragged himself on his buttocks until he was at the edge of his seat, his long legs bending at an angle. He rubbed his hands together and passed them over his face.

"We think she's missing, sir. We don't know for sure what happened, but she's not here. I arrived late..." He stopped at the word 'late' and winced. He berated himself. If only he hadn't been late. If only those hoodlums hadn't followed him. If only—

"And?" Harif probed.

Ameera sucked in air and exhaled, her chest shrinking

and returning to normal. Aisha sniffed, and Zainab shifted in her seat.

"I arrived late, and she wasn't here. Zainab said she heard a car honk and the gates open. She assumed I had arrived. Asiya's phone is still here." He lifted the phone a fraction and then dropped it. Repeating what had become his worst nightmare made his body boil. His mind went to the men who had followed him. A tiny voice in his head was screaming that the two incidents were related. He shooed it, determined not to allow it to make him feel worse.

Harif stroked his almost nonexistent beard absent-mindedly, not knowing what to think. He slumped onto the floor beside his wife, his rotund belly stretching against his striped shirt. His tie was loose, dangling at the side. His hands moved from his chin to his bald head, scratching the little hair he found.

He reached into the left pocket of his brown trousers and pulled out the old-fashioned, non-touchscreen phone he used for phone calls. He dialed Jude's number, muttering a fervent prayer that his old friend hadn't changed his number.

The two met occasionally for a cup of coffee to catch up and discuss sports and their careers. Their usual mode of communication was via email, and even that wasn't regular. However, the urgency of the matter didn't permit

Harif to attempt an email. His only option was the number his friend had given him five years ago.

Jude had been Harif's closest friend since secondary school. Even though they were in separate classes, they met after school each day to play football and talk about girls and school. Jude had always wanted to be a private investigator.

When he was younger, he spent his time watching crime documentaries, thinking up crimes in his head, and solving them. His eyes would light up and shimmer whenever he solved any of his imagined crimes or the ones featured on TV.

Young Jude's father had been murdered and robbed on the highway on his way home one evening. As the police recounted the accident to his mother, who wrung her hands in agony, Jude sat on the threshold with his lips clamped shut. Neighbors threw sympathetic looks his way, thinking he was just dumbstruck. His passion was sown in the depths of his being, mixing with grief and rage.

Later during the funeral, Jude had looked down at his father's pale and peaceful face one last time, resolving to find the murderers. He never found them, of course, but he had let no other crime go unsolved.

Jude picked up on the second ring. His excitement upon hearing from his old friend whirled past with the wind when he listened to the melancholy in Harif's voice. He agreed to see the family the following day.

Assad had to go back, but promised to return the next day. His legs felt like jelly as he walked out of the family room. His head was swimming, and leaving the family felt like a sin.

Ameera refused to go up to their bedroom even when Harif cooed and attempted to lift her. She remained gummed to the floor, rocking her body back and forth. Her breasts rested on her belly, her legs splayed, and her dress tucked clumsily between them. Her hands alternated between cupping her face and pulling her hair.

Harif sent Aisha and Zainab up to their rooms after assuring them that their dear sister would return soon. They nodded, even though they didn't believe him. Zainab kept herself from asking him to quit lying to them.

That night, Harif slept by his wife in the living room on a blanket.

CHAPTER 9

ZAINAB WOKE UP FIRST. Her older sister's absence hung over her like a damning cloud. How could they have been so careless for Asiya to have been kidnapped in broad daylight? Hours had passed since the kidnapping, but it felt like an eternity without her sister. Zainab had felt lighter when she slept the night and uncertainty away, so she turned face down in her bed and buried her head in the pillows—before long, even pretending to sleep invited thoughts and their ghosts. She threw off the covers and sat up, her face tender and her head smashing against itself.

After praying fajr, she returned to her bed. Her eyes fell on the books Asiya had borrowed for her from the library just a few days before the kidnapping. Zainab couldn't bring herself to read them now. She left her bed and plopped onto her desk, pulling out her pencils and sketchbook. After careful contemplation, she began to draw. She drew and doodled until the sun cast its early light through the windows.

The sun prodded Aisha awake. Her limbs grew heavy when she caught a whiff of the darkness drifting through the house. She prayed fajr and joined Zainab in her room, watching Asiya's name appear in Zainab's sketchbook over and over. A little while later, their father's head popped through the doorway, followed by his short frame. His face was rough and stubbly.

Harif didn't know what to say to the girls. They were too old to be lied to, so he tried to be as optimistic as possible when he greeted them. Try as he might, he couldn't keep the dread from slipping into his voice. He left them to attend to his wife. She had stayed up for most of the night and only slept between long, tired blinks. When the first cock crowed, she jolted awake and dragged herself to their bedroom to pray fajr with him. They sat on their prayer mats, each lost in thought and silent supplication.

Ameera had asked him if this was punishment for the grave sin she had tried to commit more than twenty years ago. He hadn't been able to answer her, for life was cruel to her; two daughters were gone, and she was drifting away from the other two.

Harif called to notify the hospital of his absence and

prepared breakfast for the family. Though their voices were missing, the silence between them was loud with their thoughts.

At nine a.m., Jude arrived at the Abdullah household. He was let in by Harif, who was overcome with grief but had to maintain a tough front. His family needed to know their strength hadn't been sucked out just yet. They shook hands and shared a firm embrace before heading to the family room.

Harif offered his friend coffee even before Jude could take off his suit jacket and touch a seat with his buttocks. Jude obliged, noting how Harif seemed to have aged since they last met. They were age mates, forty-six years old at present, but his friend's face showed raggedness, exhaustion, and worry.

To Harif, Jude looked almost the same as he had five years ago. He was still the tall, dark man with a slightly hunched back and a steady stride. Jude's clear eyes that saw the littlest of details hadn't lost their sharpness. His hair was, as usual, cropped short and neat, his mustache its usual long length. The only things different about his appearance were the few threads of grey hair he didn't attempt to conceal and the crow's feet that formed around his small eyes when he smiled.

The family gathered, and Jude sat facing them. He looked each of them over, feeling sorry for Ameera when his eyes found her. She visibly looked like she was retreating into herself. Jude sighed. He knew about Harissa; he had tried to aid the couple in trying to find her all those decades ago.

Assad arrived just as Jude pulled out a notebook from the black briefcase he had brought. Zainab recognized the sound of the car horn, and Harif rushed out to let him in. Assad joined the family, settling beside Aisha.

Jude began by asking each of them questions about Asiya. He asked if they knew a place she'd likely be hiding at; if she was depressed or troubled; if she hinted at leaving home; if anyone disliked her enough to harm her. Everyone answered in negation.

Next, he asked if anyone encountered anything out of the ordinary before her disappearance was discovered. Assad perked up, the memory of the people who tailed him presenting itself to him, and so he relayed this information to Jude, not missing one detail.

The family's fear heightened, and Jude closed his eyes, lost in thought. When he opened his eyes, he asked the family and Assad if they knew of anyone who opposed the couple's relationship. They shook their heads, turning their necks to look at one another to be sure.

Jude then checked Asiya's phone for anything that could be amiss. When nothing could be pulled from it, he thanked the family for seeing him and stood up to leave, straightening his burgundy tie. He grabbed his jacket and briefcase saying goodbye, unable to look Ameera in the eye. He hadn't been able to help her once, and he'd be damned if he failed her yet again.

The eerie silence returned in full force after Jude left, disrupted only by Ameera's hardly audible whimpering.

Harif started a conversation about Asiya and all the things she loved. The girls cited situations where she was hilarious, and they all laughed. The atmosphere lightened for a while but returned to somber when Ameera asked in a small voice where they thought she was, what she was doing and thinking, and how she was being treated.

She then unraveled the end of her headscarf to cover her eyes as if to hide the unbearable pain tearing her apart.

IN THE DAYS THAT FOLLOWED, life was slowly siphoned out of the Abdullah household. Space was built up like a giant monolith between the parents and their children. Aisha and Zainab constantly looked for opportunities to be alone from each other and their parents. Ameera spiraled in and out of wellness, and Harif tried to keep her in the throes of good health and have a firm grip on the entire family. Ameera stopped cleaning, and when the girls didn't cook, they bought outside food.

Despite fearing for his life, Assad visited every other day since he still had days left from his thirty-six-day sabbatical. When it ended and he returned to work, he made sure to drop by after his shift. Returning to his apartment after visiting the Abdullah family, Assad drowned in his thoughts and chided himself for doing nothing to help find her. There wasn't much he could do, though. Jude had asked him to put his safety first because those men who tailed him were bound to notice and come after him again if Assad started looking.

His lover's disappearance was taking a toll on him, so much so that his friend and coworker, Khaled, had noticed. Assad kept zoning out again and again at work, and Khaled, determined to get to the heart of the matter, decided to confront Assad.

Khaled had walked into Assad's cubicle to find piles of paperwork untouched on the table. Assad was sitting with his back to his desk and his eyes on the wall. Khaled stood there for a moment and glanced at the wall, thinking he'd find something interesting. He found nothing. His friend was in another place.

"Assad!"

Assad started and was thrown out of his reverie. He swiveled his chair to face his desk and Khaled. It was the fourth day after Jude's visit, and the man didn't have any substantial information yet.

He looked at Khaled, his friend since primary school, with a frown of worry etched on his face.

"Dude, don't look at me like that. I didn't mean to startle you, but I just saved your ass. You wouldn't want the boss to find you like this, would you?" Khaled's lips curved into an impish smile.

Assad was still looking at Khaled, but he wasn't particularly listening or thinking about Asiya or anything else. He was just absent-minded.

"Assad?" Khaled was worried. This was the third time in a week that he had caught his friend daydreaming. It had happened on Monday at lunchtime when they were discussing football, and again the next day during a staff meeting.

Whatever was bothering his friend was serious as hell if he kept losing concentration when his job depended on it. Worse, Assad looked like he hadn't been sleeping a lot lately. His eyes were dull, and his face looked like it was drooping. Anyone who had known Assad for years would know on sight that something was wrong.

"Assad!"

Assad shook his head and offered a weary smile.

"What's up, man? How long have you been standing there?"

Khaled looked at him in bewilderment.

"Long enough to watch you tune out and know you're not yourself. What the hell is going on, man?"

"Not now, not now. I'll tell you when the time is right."

Khaled was not convinced and proved it by remaining in front of Assad.

"I'll tell you when the time is right," Assad repeated.

"Okay, if you insist. But don't turn to the wall again. I won't be able to survive in this place alone if you get fired."

They laughed, but Assad's laugh—a low rumbling sound that arose from his belly—died right after exiting his mouth. Khaled looked hard at him and decided to watch his friend from afar.

"Catch you later," he said, stepping out of Assad's cubicle.

The family made efforts to immerse themselves in joy, even if it was only a mouthful. The walls of the house, however, echoed with the absence of the eldest daughter.

Jude called often, but he wasn't making any headway. He and the family marveled at how they hadn't received ransom texts or calls. If Asiya had been kidnapped, her captor clearly wanted nothing from them.

Ameera slunk around the house, avoiding places her daughter had frequented, like the her room, the seat in the kitchen Asiya often took for meals, or her lounging place on the sofa as she scrolled through her phone. To forget her troubles for a short while, Ameera resumed cleaning. She cleaned every corner of the house almost every day—except Asiya's room—and cooked more meals than the family could eat. She delegated that task to Aisha and

Zainab, who, despite their unwillingness, did it anyway. They didn't think they could handle their mother if they refused to.

The least sound caused her to jump and have outbursts. Whenever she was alone, she wallowed in distorted and disturbing thoughts about herself.

Her mind kept taking her to the year she felt a part of her die. Each time the events started playing out in their sequential order, she grabbed a broom or dashed to the kitchen.

Of course, she kept this from her husband. She was at a loss on how to tell him that her past was knocking on their door louder than ever before. In her moments of wellness, she pitied him. He would break if she told him, even if he never showed it.

Almost everything in the house was now a portal to the intrusive thoughts and gut-wrenching memories. Harif implored Dr. Davis to make his visits regular. Ameera's episodes were dormant, but he could feel his wife slipping away even more. He didn't know how to talk to her about it without her having more breakdowns, so he left the task to the doctor.

Despite trying hard, Doctor Davis couldn't get through to her. She insisted she was fine even when her lip crumpled while saying it.

The nightmares were the absolute worst. It took a lot

for her to stumble into sleep, and the moment she did, beads of sweat gathered on her face and body, wetting her dress. The faces were the same. Faces she had tried hardest to forget all these years. They beckoned to her, dark holes in place of their eyes. Then, a rip in her body and the blood-curdling cry of a baby.

She always woke up when the baby cried, her hands flying to her mouth and her eyes watering while she found her husband snoring gently beside her. She had the urge to shake him awake and cry lying on his chest, but she refused to give in. Her mind went to what would have happened next after the baby's cry, and she shuddered despite the warm room and the sweat sticking to her skin.

This cross was hers alone, and she wasn't going to let Harif carry it.

The following day, she was seated with Harif and their children in the living room when Asiya's unused slippers appeared in her line of view. Her vision blurred, and the faces returned, this time with their real eyes. They faded out, and she saw Asiya's face. Bile rose and spread in her chest and throat, rushing her to the bathroom on the ground floor.

Aisha and Zainab exchanged knowing and doleful glances as their father dropped the newspaper he was perusing and went after her. He found her huddled in the left corner of the bathroom, close to the toilet. The moment he got there, her chest heaved, and she gripped the toilet seat, emptying the contents of her stomach again. She wished the contents of her nightmares would join those of her stomach in the toilet.

"I'm a terrible mother—a horrible person. I don't deserve to live. And I don't deserve you. Any of you."

"No, no. you're sweet and kind. The best mother our children could ever ask for. Harissa too. You did what was best for her, remember? That's what a mother does. You're the love of my life, and my wife. You deserve us, and you deserve to live."

"No."

"Yes, Ameera."

Harif rubbed her back and made soothing sounds while she wiped her mouth time and again, desiring that the nightmares be wiped away. She dissolved into a puddle of salty, hot tears, and Harif couldn't hold it in any longer. He cried, his face nestled in her disheveled hair as their bodies synchronously racked.

IT'S BEEN two weeks since my capture. I can tell now that I am in a room with windows and timely meals.

I used to stay in my room all day, feeling like I was being ripped to shreds. Things have changed in the past week, though. Each day, I wake up and say my prayers and survive. I don't like it here, but at least it's bearable now.

Sometimes I feel like I wouldn't have survived this long in this house if I hadn't crossed paths with Lila. I could even say we're friends now. She's super dutiful where I'm concerned, and we're getting along just fine. It makes me wish I had an elder sister. And I don't mean Harissa. Someone else, like Lila.

I haven't seen Mr. Debayo since the first night. I recall Lila saying he is away on a business trip. Her voice wavered as she said it, like she didn't believe it at all herself.

After my first encounter with her—it's more like my second—I did what anyone in my situation would do. I thought of escaping. And the more I thought out plans, the more I realized I would have to befriend Lila. That was going to be hard; I'd never made an effort to befriend anyone before.

In all my years of having friends, people befriended me because they thought I was cool and beautiful. And sometimes, I doubted they were real friendships. They felt like popularity contracts—everyone wanted to be seen with the beautiful girl.

They hung out with me and listened to whatever I had to say, even when sometimes I knew I was talking crap, but they nodded and laughed anyway. Afterward, they spread rumors about me.

Another side of the story is that I never actually wanted to be friends with anyone. I thought of myself as being better than them, so they had to grovel for my friendship.

I was also wary of all the girls who tried so hard to be called my friends. After talking to me, some would sit with other people and suck their teeth while narrating something I said. They never hid the fact that they always wished to be me or hoped I woke up one day with a disfigured face.

I didn't mention it outright that I wanted to escape; I just hinted at it. I asked Lila questions like: if I could go out of the house, if I could get a phone, and if there were eyes that would follow my every step. She never really replied. Most of the time, she nodded or shook her head. Soon, I gave up and went back to ignoring her. That way, I wouldn't have to try befriending her, or so I thought.

I grew lonely and forced myself to deal with my arrogance. I made genuine efforts to be nice to her and talk to her.

A week into my stay here, Lila spoke more than her usual four sentences. Yes, I had been counting. That is what you do when you are being held captive, and the only thing keeping you from taking your own life is the faint glimmer of hope that one day, you will be free. She spoke a total of four sentences to me every day.

It was always the same four sentences, too: good morning, ma'am, your breakfast is ready, should I bring your lunch up here, supper is ready ma'am. Believe me, I have tried countless times to get her to stop calling me 'ma'am.' She said her boss would skin her alive if he heard her calling me by my first name as he deemed it disrespectful.

I told her it was ridiculous, as she looks like she's older than I am. She did not say anything in response, and neither did she stop calling me 'ma'am.' It irked me, but I had no choice but to accept it. Acceptance is becoming the norm for me here, so I let it be.

Anyway, she said more than her usual four sentences *and* called me by my name. She asked if she could return to my room after sending the supper tray to the kitchen. I was shocked, but I obliged.

She returned, and I asked her to make herself comfortable. She did, and my curiosity grew. I wondered what had inspired this change in a person who couldn't even look me in the eye for the past week.

She smiled—a gorgeous smile, I must add—and said she wanted to be friends. I smiled too. She was the first to say that to me.

I wondered what Mother would say about having a friend like Lila, and my face retreated into glumness. She asked if I was thinking of my family at that very moment, and I nodded.

She left the couch to sit with me on the bed and held my hands. Without any warning, tears I didn't know I had anymore escaped my eyes. She let go of my hands and pulled me into a thick embrace. I bawled, allowing myself to dissolve.

After I pulled out of the embrace, red-eyed and embarrassed, I apologized, avoiding her kind eyes. I can't exactly tell what happened after, but I knew I had a new friend—a true friend. Now I cringe every time I remember my initial rudeness towards her, and my face grows hot with embarrassment.

In the days that followed, Lila would sit with me in my room when she didn't have any chores. We would watch shows on the television and talk at length about things that excite us and things that make us want to hit something, all the while avoiding the mention of our families.

I suspected she had lost her family after she told me she's been living with Mr. Debayo for five years. Anytime she mentioned him, her face clouded.

She fed me stories about him—the people he murdered, his 'business,' and his sickening way of doing things. She told me I was lucky to be staying in my room all day because to survive in the house, one must be a recluse of sorts. The thought of escaping was slipping into the farthest corners of my mind. I still wanted to see my family and Assad again, but I didn't want to do anything that would give that monster a cause to hurt them.

I grew restless, however, and itched to walk in the gardens I could see from my window. Lila promised to walk with me.

We walked in the gardens when the other workers were indoors. Lila said it was safer that way. I didn't entirely understand what she meant by *safer*, but I didn't probe. I felt better and freer. I was still a prisoner, but being outdoors was less suffocating.

I observed the style of the house, and soon, I could walk around when she was busy. Even though I steered clear of the others, I couldn't avoid them. I bumped into them and could often feel someone stare at me even long after I passed by them.

Lila told me she heard them whispering about me, even when all I did was nod and smile when I saw any of them. I bumped into an older woman more often. She was small and always wore a grey dress with frayed ends. Her beaded eyes seemed to want to look deep inside me, and I felt she bumped into me intentionally. Lila said she's called Mari and led a man to his unprepared grave.

Friendship or not, I grew uncomfortable with Lila being my help, but she wouldn't let me do anything myself. Sometimes, I changed my bed sheets and cleaned my room and bathroom before she came up to do it. She didn't approve and asked me over and over with a stiff upper lip to let her do it, but I didn't care. Eventually, she stopped asking.

CHAPTER 12

LILA

MY DAYS here have improved since the space between Asiya and I closed up. I don't even call her 'ma'am' anymore, though I suspect I will when the boss returns.

He's on a 'business' trip and will be back in a fortnight, when a truck filled with girls aged eighteen or lower will arrive in the wee hours of the morning. They will be marched to the basement and locked up before being moved to the warehouse in the next town and then shipped off to Kenya or another country.

While they are here, we will be charged with cooking tasteless food for them. They only need to stay alive, not fatten up like pigs. The boss's henchmen will feed them in the morning and evening.

Some of the luckier ones will die here. Luckier,

because death is worth more than slaving away for some potbellied men or being their sex objects.

I don't like to think about what happens to those poor girls. I'm not certain if it's them working and being beaten like animals or them being subjected to other kinds of perversion those men have that makes me want to retch. Or that the men who get these girls are the same filthy rich men who donate to orphanages and create foundations for employment with smug and satisfied smiles.

Hundreds of girls go missing each year, and after a few weeks of searching for them, their cases are abandoned. None of those girls deserve it...nobody deserves the terrible things life throws them.

I left Asiya's room a while ago. The glumness has been lifted off her face, but she still doesn't eat much. I hope she isn't losing weight. I find it amusing how I worry about her like she's my sister. I'm back in the kitchen washing dishes.

I never imagined having a friend after Bella and Ruth in this house, no less. I smile and laugh a lot now, and even though I get looks from the other workers, I don't care.

This new friendship I'm enjoying has its encumbrances. I've been catching myself longing for a life outside these walls. I mean, I used to, but I had already resigned to the fact that I may never leave. It's different now. I long for freedom and connections, and a life of my own. I long for a home and belonging.

And I know this may sound like me acting out of character, but I've started looking for weaknesses in this house. Anything that could serve as a means of escape. I have found none.

The gates are locked almost all the time, and if we do manage to get to the gate, we'll be shot at best. We are just discardable bodies like all those that have found eternal homes in the ground—even Asiya. The boss wanting to keep her as his trophy doesn't make her any safer than I am.

I have considered the walls also. They are incredibly high—and worse—there are electric wires slithering along their lengths. To attempt to jump them would be suicide, and as I said, I like living.

I don't go out often, but when I do, I'm watched by invisible eyes who will report to the boss even when he's not in town. In all my years of staying here, I don't know the name of this town. I don't even know if it has one.

It's a small town, but everyone minds their business even when they see strange things. It's no surprise they act as though the mansion doesn't exist.

If we manage to escape and the cronies track us down in the town, I know everyone would look away. They would pretend they can't see us being dragged back to the mansion.

On the inside, the servants look for ways to gain favor with the boss, and they will gladly serve my lifeless body to him if it will help them survive better. The boss does what he can to make my life miserable by reminding me of Baba and Mami, but I'm the one who's usually asked to go on errands. I suppose it's because I have no friends whatso-ever—or used to. Or because the boss knows I wouldn't do anything stupid out of fear for my life.

And he's right. Except now that Asiya is here with me, the desire to be free has seared my senses, and I can't help but think of escape plans. Asiya has no idea, though, and I plan to keep it that way. Until I'm ready.

I suddenly feel that I'm being watched, and my neck whips toward the kitchen entrance. Oh, it's only T-Bone. He's the monster's right-hand man, a demon himself. He carries out the master's dirty deeds when he's out of town. The first time I heard his name, I swear I almost choked on my laughter. I mean, what sort of name is T-Bone? I know it's a nickname, but still, what the hell? Is it supposed to make people fear him? He doesn't need a nickname for that. His face is enough to make anyone think twice about pissing him off.

I rinse my hands in the sink and look T-Bone in the eye. As much as I keep to myself, I try to never allow any of these liars and murderers to intimidate me. I force myself never to look away when I can look them in the eye.

During moments like this, what happened to my

parents fuels my strength. He stares me down, and I match him, starting from the top of his egg-shaped head down to his face. A ghost of a tight smile plays at my lips, but I keep my eyes cold and unwavering.

T-Bone wears the same thing every day—jeans and a shirt that is too tight with a shotgun holstered in the hem of the jean. Sometimes, I want to scream at him to change his clothes. I don't, though. He has a reputation for hitting women and enjoying it.

My eyes hover on his face. He has an ugly scar running from his left eyebrow down his cheek, and his right eye has a patch over it.

These are the scars the master gave him with his powdered hands when he failed an assignment. He immersed a flat metal in fire and burned T-Bone's right eye with it, laughing deep from his throat all the while. A month later, he used a knife to carve the scar into T-Bone's face. T-Bone hasn't failed ever since.

He's also the only male who works here who never allows himself a joint or shot—aside from the boss. T-Bone says weed and alcohol make him sloppy, and his job is too important to be botched. Every time he reiterates his reason for forsaking the bottle and drugs, his fingers graze his scars as if to remind him they're there.

He cocks his head and stares right through me with his

left eye. I fear he can hear the loudness of my heart when it slams against my chest, albeit my putting on a defiant mask. Or he can see the thoughts of escape gliding without a care in the world in my troubled mind. This one scares me the most.

He finally breaks the stare, and his fingers brush the gun in its holster.

"You have to go out alone today. We need some material to wrap any dead bodies we may have any day from today."

I almost jump out of my skin when his voice cuts through the silence. Materials, huh? I hope he dies with them. But I could never say it to him, or I'd die first.

"Okay," I croak.

The hardness on his face transforms into self-satisfaction at the sound of my voice. Damn it. My voice has betrayed my face.

"You know the rules," he drawls. "Buy what you need and get your pretty ass back here. The streets have eyes and ears." His eyes take in my body, and he slowly licks his thick dark lips before he turns to leave.

This is the hundredth time I've had to endure his lusty gazes and comments. I detest him even more for it. The other female servants swear they hate it, too, until they find themselves lying splayed in his bed. It takes no genius to figure out he has been sleeping with them. One day, they abhor him, and the next, they sing praises of him.

Who in their right mind would eulogize T-Bone? The boss, maybe. But even he's careful not to rub his pet demon's ego too much.

I leave the kitchen when his footsteps fade out and head to my room.

I change into a pair of faded jeans and a t-shirt. I look in the mirror and smooth my hair before tying it with a black scarf. I head out and find T-Bone standing by the gates, one leg angled with his foot resting on the wall. He crosses his arms and stares at me as I approach him. I pretend to remove dirt from my nails to avoid his gaze.

He opens the gate and starts whistling when I'm within earshot. I step out of the house and breathe in the air that suddenly feels different. I trudge quickly but carefully, avoiding eyes and sticking to the deserted parts of the road.

I keep my gaze on the ground and come to a halt when a familiar form appears before me, holding out a small basket of potatoes.

I smile and clear my throat, pretending to check them out. This is our plan. Zayn always surprises me.

I met Zayn the first time I was sent on an errand alone almost a year ago. I had sensed that I was being followed and ducked into the materials shop. The stalker followed and stood right behind me, initiating a conversation while sifting through products like he was there to buy something.

He said he'd seen two dangerous-looking people watching my every move, and he wanted to warn me. I thanked him and assured him I was safe, which, of course, he didn't believe. And so, our conversation continued.

I think I'd call the conversation one-sided because I only told him my name and that I lived in the town, too, while he went on to tell me his name, talked about his family a bit, and his education.

It felt good in a weird sort of way, knowing someone was genuinely interested in talking to me. After I bought my material, he bought some, too. When I asked him why he bought it, he'd said he didn't trust that I was safe, and so he was just pretending. My face felt hot, and I thought of him as sweet.

I thought it sweetest when he maintained his distance all the time while talking to me to keep things halal. We weren't engaged or married, and he was a non-mahram, so it was religious of him to do so when many others wouldn't think twice about little details like that. His sweetness toward me wasn't just restricted to our first meeting.

The second time we met, he came over to me with a basket of potatoes he got from God knows where. He said people were still watching me—different people—and the potatoes would be his way of talking to me. I looked around, uneasy, and screamed in my head for not being free to have a normal life.

On that day, he asked me if I lived in 'rich man's mansion'. I found it funny, and I laughed until I snorted. I couldn't lie to him for reasons I still cannot fathom, and I knew my honesty pained him. He asked over and over if I was happy and safe. He said he'd try to get me out of there, but I politely declined his offer. I hope I can introduce him to Asiya in better conditions.

Now, here we are, together again. I don't know whether to call him a friend because of how warm I feel whenever I see him.

I ask him how he knew I was out of the house and hope my voice didn't give away my excitement. He said he paid a little boy with toffees to run as fast as his legs could carry him each time he saw me walk in the direction of the market.

Zayn lives close to the market with his family in a house I haven't seen. He says it's a small, unpainted house with old, weathered roofing and not much to look at. As a web developer, he works from home and likes to walk around town when there isn't much to do.

He seems to grow taller each time I see him, and today is no different. He looks at me, his lanky figure slouching slightly. He has on his charming boyish smile and rakes his fingers through his afro every few minutes.

I still pretend to be interested in the potatoes while we walk to the materials shop. He then abandons the basket in the shop of the woman he borrowed it from, and takes his usual place behind me when we get to the shop.

It's just the two of us in the shop today, and the old man who owns the shop has stepped outside for a moment. Before I can think twice about it, I turn to Zayn, and the words leave my mouth: "I want to escape."

He looks taken aback, with eyes wide in silence. I've never wanted to even discuss leaving my bondage. He recovers seconds later, and a grin forms on his face. I look away. I shouldn't be feeling this way. What if he doesn't like me?

"Well, well, well," he says. His voice is low, and his eyes are twinkling in mischief. "It's about time."

I roll my eyes and laugh. He joins in, not ready to peel his eyes off my face. My heartbeat quickens, and I become all too aware of the way we're close.

"Do you have a plan?" His question makes the awkwardness lift and hang high above our heads.

"No," I say. I chew on my bottom lip, and my belly feels funny.

"We'll figure it out," he says.

We. The funny feeling again.

His smile is so assuring. I want to believe for a moment that I'll be free. Allow myself to ride on dreams and hopes even if it could all catch fire, and I'll be left with nothing. Without my life, even.

Here and now, with him, I'll dream and hope for a silhouette of home.

CHAPTER 13

JUDE WAS DROWNING in coffee by the gallons and losing sleep but was still not making any headway on the Abdullah case. Until Assad's phone call. He was sitting at his desk in his home office, ruminating once more on the story the family had narrated, when his phone rang.

He hesitated—it was nine p.m., and he didn't recognize the caller's number. He picked up his cell phone slowly and toggled the answer button. He remained silent, waiting for the caller to speak up first.

At the other end was heavy breathing. He drummed his fingers on his oak table—his patience was thinning out, and fast.

"Hello?" the voice at the other end said. It sounded vaguely familiar. He had probably met the person in passing. "Hello, sir. This is Assad speaking."

Jude perked up at the name.

"Assad. How's it going?" He knew something was wrong for the young man to call him at that hour, but it was always best to let them speak first.

"Sir, I'm in trouble. I stopped by the mall to get a few items. I saw a masked person aiming a gun at me as I was exiting the mall. I ducked, and he shot someone else. I got in my car, and now I'm being tailed." There was a tremor in Assad's voice, and his labored breathing grew more tense by the minute.

"How many men do you think are there?" Jude was already pulling on a coat and strapping two pistols to his trousers.

"Just one, sir."

"And where are you?"

"I'm driving on the Green Highway now."

"Good, I'm close by. Keep driving. My boys and I will creep up on him from behind."

"Yes, sir." Assad stopped short of mentioning how terrified he was and how he had already tried and failed to prepare for the possibility of death.

"What color is your car?"

"Grey."

"And our man? What's the color of his car?"

"Black."

"Right. See you."

Jude called his old friend, the chief police officer, and explained the situation. The latter dispatched three men to aid Jude and give chase to the assailant.

They soon spotted the two cars, one tailing the other closely. Jude called Assad and asked him to turn to a dead-end road and slow down. Assad did. The assailant also had no choice but to slow down, and the moment he did, Jude and the police brought their cars to a halt.

They jumped out of their seats and approached the car, surrounding it before the driver could escape. Jude and the other police officers approached the car, their pistols poised at the ready, as the black car door flew open. They were met with the driver's hard and remorseless face, and his hand gripped his own pistol. Jude whistled and shook his head.

The assailant dropped his weapon and raised his hands high above his head. Jude stepped closer, kicking the pistol farther away. A policeman forced the assailant's arms behind him and cuffed his hands.

Jude, noticing how shaken Assad seemed, told him to go home and that everything was taken care of. Assad obliged, getting into his car and driving off.

The police and Jude drove to the police station and uncuffed the assailant, throwing him in the interrogation room. Jude sat opposite him and regarded him for a couple of seconds—his dirty dreadlocks, dark lips and bloodshot eyes, the heavy scent of tobacco on him.

"Go ahead, then, kill me," he said, his voice ragged, icy, and angry. "I no go tell you anything. All you coti fit burn!" His eyes held venom that threatened to spill onto the table between him and Jude.

Jude knew, then, the kind of man the criminal was— the same kind of men who worked for Debayo—men who lived their entire lives on the streets, with little to no education.

When Jude remained calm and unruffled, the criminal continued, "I go die before I go talk. Kill me chale. E go better say I die than I go talk."

Jude wiped a speck of spit that had landed on his cheek when the assailant was speaking. His lips tilted into a slight smile, and his eyes remained still. "Relax, friend. Nobody is going to kill you. Not yet, anyway. But if you keep this up, you're the one who's going to burn, I assure you." Jude paused. "All that will be prevented if you tell me who put you on the job. Your boss. His name, his whereabouts. You'll be protected and given fewer years in prison."

"You fit open my moff you no go hear nothing." Despite the strong words, his voice shook now, and he panted.

"You're talking now, and I haven't pried your lips open. But you're not telling me what I want to know. You don't want to force me to resort to more...gruesome methods, do you, friend?"

"I no be your paddy. I tell you norr I be dead person."

"At least you're thinking about it, whether you admit it or not. Think about your family, Mister...?"

"Ben." He sniffed at the mention of his family, and his dirty and poorly maintained nails scratched the skin of his neck.

"Mr. Ben. Think about your family, will you? My men are looking for them as we speak. Do them a favor and prolong your life, pal. You can always start over." Jude smiled again, the ends of his lips straining to reach his ears now.

Ben looked at Jude, fear crisscrossed on his angular face. The scar above his left eyebrow seemed to pulsate in the dimmed lighting of the interrogation room. His thumb and forefinger reached up to press into his eyes in an attempt to clean the tears forming in them.

"Okay," he finally said. Ben kept his eyes on the table, and drops of tears fell on it. "But you for keep your promise. I die saf lef my family, you for protect am."

"You have my word, Ben. No harm will come to your family. I knew we could work together!" Jude clapped once and let out a laugh.

"One more thing."

"Go on."

"I fit get some water?"

"Of course. I'll go get it." Jude locked the interrogation room from the outside and left.

He returned with a bottle of water and let out a curse when his eyes adjusted once more to the dimness of the room. Ben was sprawled on the metal table, foaming at the mouth.

"Bastard!" Jude yelled. He grabbed the little bottle in Ben's hand and squinted at it. They didn't see it when they searched him for hidden weapons. It was almost empty of the colorless liquid in it. He brought it to his nose and set it back on the table when he couldn't identify its smell.

Jude kicked the chair he sat on earlier, the muscles in his face contracting with each yelled curse. He should have checked the assailant's body for substances like this. The worst part was going to be breaking the news to Assad and Harif.

He called for the forensic team to take away the body and slammed his car door as he entered it. Jude's lips twisted as he stared at the dark, headlight-lit road in front of him to turn the car toward the Abdullah residence.

The family and Assad remained quiet all throughout Jude's narration. Harif and Ameera seemed to have aged beyond their years, and their children lacked their usual refreshing spark and excitement. They sighed and shook their heads, holding on to each other. But Jude could sense it—they were giving up on ever seeing Asiya again.

I HAVE FOUND a way to escape. At least, I think I have. I've been going on more errands of late, and even though I think it's strange, I welcome each opportunity with open arms. I get to see Zayn and get away from the madness in this house.

I know I've lived here for years, but it doesn't make it any less stifling. I dream of freedom in the mornings and nights, so I've taken it as a sign. I still haven't told Asiya yet. I will when Zayn and I have finalized the arrangements.

I often wonder what'll happen if I escape—with Zayn, I mean. He has grown so much on me that it'll be hard to pretend he doesn't exist when I'm out of here.

He's the closest thing I've gotten to loving someone after Adam. I usually stay up at night, imagining alternate days. Days when I won't be a single twenty-six-year-old stuck within the confines of a repulsive man.

I probably shouldn't be thinking about this, but I'm lucky where the pressure to get married is concerned. I'm invisible, hidden in plain sight. Not many people speak to me, never mind asking me my age or why I don't have a husband yet. So yes, I *am* lucky. Not every twenty-six-year-old gets to live a life devoid of hearing the voice of self-acclaimed aunties in her head every day— voices incessantly talking about marriage and children and womanhood.

I want to marry the love of my life one day and start a family without the unnecessary pressure from the loud women who pretend they don't need to be saved from their abusive marriages by meddling in others'. The irony is not lost on me—most of these community aunties are not happy in their marriages but never pass up an opportunity to tell a young girl to give up her dreams and get married. I often wonder: do they want others to share their misery, or is there is something else? Perhaps they think the dream of a perfect marriage they were sold on could be sold to someone else.

First things first. When I get out, I'll see about returning to school to compensate for my lost years. Mami and Baba would want that.

I'm on my way back to the mansion after an errand. I

wonder what would happen if I left the steak by the metal gates and ran for my life. No doubt, seemingly normal people will draw up pistols hidden in their clothes and fire before I take another step.

I get to the gates and rap sharply twice. Our part of town is deserted, a dusty narrow road with sickly plants sprouting from the brown ground. Our house is the only one I can see now.

I would have to walk a few more miles to see the next one. A second later, the gate opens only a bit, and T-Bone's smirk comes into view. Just looking at him makes me sick, but he's the boss after the boss. The slightest act of defiance would earn me a bullet, or worse.

I squeeze past him and make my way to the kitchen. I dump the steak on the kitchen counter and climb the stairs to Asiya's room. I knock on the door once, so she knows it's me. She opens the door, a toothy grin on her face.

I'm smiling, too, in no time—that's the effect she has on me.

"Look at you being all smiley," she says, sitting on her bed. "Did the errand go well, or has T-Bone learned how to be a gentleman?"

"Shhh! Someone could hear you. Do you want a more miserable life than the one you have already?" My index finger rests on my lips as I speak.

"Relax. Nobody would hear us. Who cares what we

have to talk about, anyway?" She rolls her eyes and tosses a book across the bed. She leaves the chair and sits cross-legged opposite me on the floor.

I shake my head. She doesn't know what she's talking about.

"So, don't change the topic. What has got you smiling like that?"

I laugh. "I don't know. When you opened the door, you had this wide grin on your face. Who wouldn't smile at that, hmm?"

"Oh no. No way. Don't blame it on me, missy. You literally skipped from the door to this place." She sticks her finger into the carpet. "I've observed you for a while now. There's a bounce in your steps. Maybe it's always been there, and I'm just noticing it. But I want to know. What has got miss-I-always-keep-to-myself to be so warm?"

I laugh again. Deep down, I don't know if I should tell her about Zayn. It's nice to have someone to share your feelings and thoughts with, but it's a death sentence if that someone is the wrong person.

"Or is it a who?" she gasps. "It *is* a who!" Her gaze latches expectantly onto mine.

"Okay, fine." I raise my hands in mock surrender and sit next to her, gauging her face for a reaction. "It's a who."

Her eyes widen and sparkle, and she has a hard time wiping the smile off her face. "My day just got made. Who is he? How did you meet? Where is he from? I want to know everything! I wish we had some fruit juice for this, but let's make do without it. Now, spill."

"He's—erm. We haven't...you know, erm. Well, I—" Wow, I had no idea talking about him would be so hard. I can't even get the words to form.

"Take a deep breath," she says. "Start from wherever you want. No pressure."

I take a deep breath and smoothen my black dress. "We're not...together. We've only met a few times. When I go out on errands...He's named Zayn. He's a sweet person."

She grins again and grabs my hands. "Look at you. Your face altered when you were talking. I could actually feel the warmth of your face. And your eyes! They went dreamy and wide."

I try to hide my face, embarrassed. It feels good doing this—talking about him—and I can't help but wonder once again what would happen if I left.

"But you *do* like him, right?"

"Of course," I say. My eyes are still downcast.

"And why aren't you together?"

"Well, what with me being here...it's not safe. And he hasn't said anything. For all I know, it could be one-sided."

"Oh no. I doubt it. I haven't seen it, but I doubt it. Hold on to it—whatever you're feeling. Okay?"

I decide to leave her room and retreat to my room, ready to nurse my thoughts and allow them to swallow me whole. I pray maghreb and then wait for isha—I've started praying regularly now because she encouraged me to.

After praying, I lie sprawled on my mattress, and just as sleep is about to consume me, I hear voices outside my door, and I can clearly make out T-Bone's. I listen intently, sleep going away as quickly as it had swooped down on me. My curiosity is piqued nonetheless—I haven't heard anything out of the ordinary of late. I hear the cries of a woman begging to be spared.

I sit up and prop a hand on my knee, my ears straining to listen. She is weeping now, and I hear T-Bone ask her to shut up. There are other male voices, ones I cannot identify. I assume they belong to the other guards.

I step out of my room, restless. I wonder who is so unfortunate to have to beg T-Bone for her life. I go up to Asiya's room and knock once. I hear the lock click, and the door pulls open to reveal a panic-stricken Asiya. Her saucer eyes bore into mine, and she asks questions I have no reply for.

I sit cross-legged on the floor, and she perches on the edge of the bed, eyes darting to the windows now and then. There's a sudden quiet, and before we can get used to it, we hear gunshots.

Asiya's hand flies to her mouth, and the blood drains

from her face as she stares at me. I stiffen even though I know the boss would let T-Bone do his dirty jobs for him in his absence, and this isn't the first one I'm witnessing. She rushes to the windows and pulls the drapery away before I can stop her. I sigh and join her. She shouldn't see or listen to this.

It's dark, but the streetlight at the edge of the garden makes it easy to see everything. A woman is splayed on the floor in her blood. T-Bone returns his pistol to its holster and bark orders at the other three guys standing near him. Two of them are smoking, and they try to drag the dead woman.

Asiya pulls the drapery back in place and backs away toward her bed. When I leave the window and look at her again, her eyes are closed, and each cheek has a tear trailing down towards her chin.

I sit in silence at the foot of the bed, lost in thought and in words unspoken. I want to console her, don't know what to say to her. I stay in her room until midnight, when she's asleep. Then, I creep out and tiptoe to my room.

I don't know when I slept, but it's already morning, and I'm awake. The previous night's events play in my brain in a loop as I shower and pray fajr.

I make my way to Asiya's room, but change my mind and go downstairs to the kitchen. I meet Mari, who's washing her hands, and pretend to look for something in the cabinets.

I want to know the details of what happened last night, but I'm almost as scared of Mari as I am of T-Bone. She volunteers the information when I stay long enough by the cabinets.

The woman prepared dinner last night and was killed because she attempted to poison the guards' food. One of T-Bone's men had chanced upon her in the kitchen and dragged her to the boys' quarters with him. Her motive? She had received information from T-Bone about her son battling death in the hospital. The poison was her attempt at escaping.

When Mari mentions the bit about the poison, I shiver visibly. I'm sure Mari notices but keeps her opinions to herself because she thinks I'm terrified about the poor woman's death.

I'm still shivering for a completely different reason. T-Bone is going to be extra careful now. We're never getting out of here.

During midday, I sit with Asiya in a spot I like to call my own: a small triangular piece of land filled with grass, weeds, and insects. It is sandwiched between the eastern wall of the mansion and place where the guards sleep. The grass is overgrown because this part of the house is mostly neglected, even by the boss, who takes note of the littlest details. Nobody ever comes here, so I've spent hours alone with my thoughts with no interruptions. Just the way I like it.

We are talking—mostly Asiya—about random stuff. I don't mind, because I enjoy listening to her talk. That's only one of three reasons why I don't talk much, though. The second reason is that I don't have much to share about my life before Debayo brought me here, while Asiya has so much to share—funny stories about her course mates and little sisters. The third reason I don't talk is that *she loves* to talk, and I'm not one to compete.

She's narrating a story about this girl in her department who has a terrible, terrible fashion sense when the gates open. We share a look and spring onto our feet, tiptoeing forward. We stand pressed to the side of the house, watching what's going on with tight lips to make sure not to be spotted. One of the many Range Rovers the boss owns speeds inside, screeching to a halt in the middle of the compound.

T-Bone jumps out, along with three other guards. Two of them drag a man out of the car and push him onto his knees. His hands are bound behind him, and his eyes and mouth are covered with pieces of white cloth. I gasp and cover my mouth, but I am too late. T-Bone has heard me.

He walks towards us, and we stay rooted in the spot. There is nowhere to run to. He sees us and sneers, looking from me to Asiya and back to me.

"Go back inside," he drawls.

I am so sure I'm visibly shaking like a leaf. Today, I can't even pretend he doesn't terrify me. I feel like he's watching me closely—too closely. Like he's reading my thoughts, and he knows I want to escape. Asiya's hand closes around mine, and it feels so reassuring. Still, it does nothing to slow my heart.

His gaze narrows on me. "You have always been timid. But you are not dumb. You know what's about to happen. Take your new friend to her room unless you want to watch someone die. Wouldn't be a first, would it?"

A tear escapes my right eye, and I grit my teeth. Asiya quickly looks at me and stands in front of me, right in his face. He doesn't spare her a glance.

"Don't talk to my friend like that," she says. She sounds fierce and confident, and I'd give anything to be like her. To be able to defend myself and her, too. But this is wrong. She shouldn't be doing this. This guy is insane; he could hurt her.

T-Bone sizes her up. "So, you are hot-headed. You would know better than to talk to me like that if you weren't. You are lucky the boss likes you. Get out of my sight."

Asiya doesn't budge. I pull her hand, but she stands her ground. She moves closer to him. "You will not treat people anyhow and get away with it. Your cup will become full, and your day of retribution will arrive sooner than you can remember this day." Her voice carries anger, and it only frightens me more. I need to get her away from him before he loses it.

"Not before I smash the cup against the wall," T-Bone says, laughing like he has lost his mind.

Asiya walks away, and I follow. When we are almost at her door, we hear three successive gunshots. She flinches with each one and stills for a moment before entering her room. She doesn't say a word the rest of the day.

FIVE YEARS AGO, and all the years before that, my life was different. Free. Safe. And all the other adjectives you can think of. In the years before I came here, Mami and Baba lived—they didn't just live. They *lived*. Our home was more than just a house; it burst at the seams with so much life.

I guess if I want to tell this story—the story of how I ended up in this princely estate with a beast as its king—I need to start from somewhere. The beginning, maybe. Let me not bore you—my life only consisted of going to school and getting bullied, loving unrequitedly, having two friends, and seeking safety and love with my parents. I suppose I should start from when things began to come undone then.

We lived in Greater Accra, thirty kilometers from the

Tema motorway. Ours wasn't the only home, though. There were about five to six other houses. Our home was not small or large, just the right size for a man, his wife, and his daughter. It was warm and cozy, with two bedrooms, one for my parents and one for me. Home smelled of essential oils, predominantly lemon and cinnamon.

Mami loved that scent, and so did our visitors. They said the smell made them wish they lived with us. My two friends, Bella and Ruth, loved coming over for the same reason. The smell is still sharp and insistent, whenever I dream of home, like I never left.

Mami said we had lived in that house ever since she became pregnant with me. She and Baba moved from another city and settled in Tema Community 12. And we lived there until everything began to come undone: when Mami fell ill.

It was quite a usual day of suffering bullies at school. I grabbed my backpack with sickening words written on it and walked fast—or almost ran home. My pace slowed when I reached the threshold of my house, and my tight chest was beginning to soften.

I beamed as I entered the living room. I could smell some soup already, and my belly growled in response. I found Mami and Baba seated so close that they were almost melting into each other. Mami was crying, and Baba rubbed her arm, his eyes moist.

I dropped my backpack on the nearest couch and sat at Mami's feet, looking up at her and Baba with confusion.

"Welcome home, little one," Baba said. He drew a hand over his face and tried to stretch his lips, but they wouldn't give. He'd been calling me 'little one' since I learned to crawl and then walk. He still called me 'little one' when my flesh grew thicker and rounder in noticeable places. He called me 'little one' even when people called me too fat or too big for my age.

"Baba," I said. I didn't know what to say or ask. I decided just to speak what words my tongue formed. "What's wrong with Mami?"

"Mami is not well, little one. We went to the hospital today and got some really bad news—"

"Let me tell her," Mami interrupted. Her voice was hoarse and broken. "Mami has got breast cancer," she said. She sniveled and buried her head in Baba's chest, a fresh wave of tears shaking her body.

I was confused and shocked all at once. Why? Mami was such a kind person. Why did this have to happen to her?

"How? When?"

"It started over a year ago, I think. I felt something in my breasts, but I ignored it. With time, my breasts changed in appearance. Your father noticed and badgered me about going to the hospital. I didn't. Then today, he took me and—" She shook her head, unable to continue.

"It's turned into full-blown cancer now, and it's spreading. The doctor said we can do chemotherapy, but it will only delay the growth, not stop it. She has about three to five years left." His voice caught as he said this, and he looked away.

Mami leaned her lithe body on Baba's stocky frame, rocking back and forth. Baba pulled her into another embrace, kissing her forehead and running his hand up and down her arm. His face remained stoic, but the occasional swelling of his chest gave his trepidation away.

I sat opposite them, thoughts darting across my mind. My face was soon wet, and my eyes pricked and burned. I had no idea when the tears escaped my eyes. We sat there until Lord knows when. I finally clambered up, my legs feeling like they could give any time, and wobbled to the small kitchen across the living room.

I warmed the soup and rice in the microwave, all the while driving my nails into my skin. I wanted to knock myself back into reality—a reality where Mami was fine, one where she'd laugh all day long, eyes squinting and glassy.

The winds blew the strength out of our home, one year at a time, and we were stuck in a rut. There was no money for the obscenely expensive chemo, and Baba's construction job just couldn't suffice. He eventually sold all the valuables he could lay hands on in our house—Mami's wedding jewelry, her expensive asoebi from Holland, the cookware still in their boxes—but none of it was enough.

And then, Baba met Debayo. I was home for the weekend and in the kitchen when Baba burst in. I had started university earlier that year with money Baba got from a friend who genuinely wanted to help us. I was also working at a bookshop close to the university, keeping the ledger organized and selling books and stationery to help cover costs.

Baba could barely keep the excitement from his voice. His eyes were glassy, and he smiled the entire time he spoke, something he hadn't done since Mami got diagnosed.

"Where's Mami?" he asked.

"She's sleeping," I answered, the curiosity jumping right out of my voice.

"Oh. I don't want to wake her up, but you won't believe what's happened."

I cleaned my wet hands with a towel and moved away from the sink and the plates I was washing. I set two stools aside, and we sat facing each other. He didn't wait for me to ask.

"I met a man. Or we met. The hospital called me about some bills, and when we were discussing the payment, this gentleman seemed to be listening to every word. I got uncomfortable and tried to convince the accountant I'd pay." He chuckled. "Well, of course, she didn't believe I'd get the money as soon as possible. I saw it in the way she twisted her face. Then, when I was leaving, I heard a cough behind me. When I turned, it was the gentleman from the office. He told me to wait."

Baba was smiling at this point. His tired eyes glinted, and the wrinkles on his face seemed to melt into his skin to bring out youth. I smiled, too; I couldn't help it.

"So, he walked with me to the front of the hospital and told me he wanted to help me. I looked at him suspiciously and asked him why. He said he's a businessman and he loves to help people in need. I was still skeptical, but he made us return to the office, where he settled the debt in front of my two eyes. Hei! I was speechless, and I thanked him over and over. But I didn't feel good about it. You know there's nothing like a free lunch. So, I told him to consider it a loan. He disagreed, but I was adamant, and he had no choice but to accept. And that's not all. He asked the accountant to alert him if we get any more bills to pay. I didn't know what to say."

"But you're still going to pay him back?" I was incredulous, the smile on my lips melting away. Unease was beginning to claw up my body, and I fidgeted on the stool.

"Yes. I asked him to give me a year."

I shook my head, not knowing what to say. "But Baba, how are you going to pay back all that money?"

"I thought about that too, but Allah will take care of us. He always does. Let's trust Him."

The unease was now squeezing my body. "Baba, we trust Allah, but we need to make realistic decisions, too."

He looked at me, fidgeting. It was as if he had just realized the graveness of what he did. "He said something else too."

I raised my eyebrows.

"He said something about not taking kindly to people who don't repay their debts. I thought it was a joke. But he said I did the smart thing by asking him to consider his benevolence a loan. And that he would've asked certain things of me if I hadn't. Things he was sure I wouldn't be able to do. But if I'm not able to pay by the stipulated time, he would punish me...."

"Punish you?" I blurted. My voice was several decibels high. "Who does he think he is?"

He held up a slender, wrinkled hand to silence me and continued. "He looked rich and powerful. I'm sure he *is* somebody. But it was the way he said it that scared me. I asked him to take his money back, but he wouldn't."

I punched my fist into my palm and stood up. "What are you going to do now?" My mouth was dry and tasted like paper.

"I'm going to take on extra jobs to pay him back."

I nodded slowly. Baba was growing older by the day. Mami's illness was taking an evident toll on him. "I'll give you ninety percent of whatever I make from the bookshop."

"No, no. That's yours. You're a woman now. You need some money on you all the time." He scratched his greying hair. "It is wrong to take it from you. I am responsible for taking care of you and your mother, but I am failing. Whatever punishment he decides to mete out, I will accept it and not drag you or your mother into it. I will never forgive myself if I do."

"Baba, please don't say that. He won't punish you. I won't let him." He looked at me with a sad smile on his lips as if he didn't believe me. "I'll manage, Baba. Please, allow me to help."

"Give me fifty percent, then. Ninety is too much. I don't want to inconvenience you. I know you won't complain even when you need money. And I think we should keep this from your mother. She's already in pain. Knowing this will make her situation worse."

I nodded, sitting back down on the stool. He held my hand, both of us lost in our thoughts.

The following year crept up on us. I was home again on a weekend when our home, hanging by a thread, was finally unwound.

Mami was taking a nap after a chemo session while I fixed something for supper. After cooking, I popped in to check on her when I noticed her chest was still. I moved closer, reasoning the stillness of her chest as a trick of the light.

I sat beside her on the bed and looked at her for what felt like an eternity. She looked peaceful, but there was no gentle rise and fall of her chest. I tried to feel her pulse—it was absent. The room wasn't hot in the least, but my face was drenched with sweat, and I could feel a wetness slide down my back. Something pulled my stomach down into the pits of my body, and I sprang to my feet.

It could not be. I placed my ear to her bosom, a maddening twitch in my eyes. My lips parted to call her name, but only a whimper escaped.

My breath was coming out in short gasps—my lungs suddenly felt too big and too bulky in my chest. I needed air. I needed help. I needed to call Baba. I needed to move my feet, but they were rooted on the spot. My body was on fire. I opened my mouth again and tasted salt—sweat or tears, I couldn't tell.

My eyes felt like they could leave their sockets, all the while pouring like a broken dam. My legs finally moved and carried me, slowly at first, and then in sprints, to Baba's workplace.

I couldn't see people's stares, but I could feel them boring into me from all angles. The only thing I could see in front of me was the blurry road leading to Baba.

I burst into his workplace and made a beeline to where he was crouched by some mortar. I stood there, teeth chattering, heart and mind threatening to burst. He looked up and instantly knew. His jaw tightened as he moved to whisper something to his colleagues. He took my hand without saying a word and led me home.

Mami was buried that same day.

When I close my eyes sometimes, I can see still the white cloth they wrapped her in, and I can make out her presence. I remember how she looked like she belonged with death—peaceful, devoid of suffering and illness—at home.

People came by to offer their condolences. Baba nodded and shook hands with some of them as they spoke of the goodness Mami had taken to the grave with her. I sat on the floor in the corner, back propped against the wall with peeling paint we hadn't the money to fix.

It wasn't just the paint that was peeling. My life and that of Baba peeled with it, falling into the dirt and getting trampled on by well-wishers.

As if Mami's death wasn't enough, Debayo came for

his money. It was time to pay up, and we hadn't recovered even fifty percent of the total amount. He visited us a week after Mami died, with his Range Rover parked out front. How he found us, we had no inkling.

Bile rose in my throat, and my skin pricked the first time I saw him. He wore a kaftan and occasionally looked at me. At a point, I felt his eyes look right through me.

Baba talked to him and tried to reason with him, but the hateful man gave him just a week to raise the remaining amount. Of course, Baba couldn't raise it, and Debayo returned.

I was painting in the living room when I heard the roar of an engine and the squelch of tires. My heart raced, and I walked into Baba's bedroom to find him sobbing. He was bent over, and his back moved with each sob.

The air shifted—he was here. He didn't knock, didn't feel the need to knock on the door of people who belonged to him. Baba dabbed his eyes almost dry and walked into the living room with me trailing behind him.

The ends of Debayo's lips tipped upwards in a cold smile. Baba went on his knees and pleaded as if his life depended on it—and it felt like it did. Debayo's hand withdrew from his kaftan, and my eyes went wild. The pistol was black, shiny, and ominous.

My cry rang in tandem with the gunshot. I sank to my knees as Baba's dark skin paled, and his blood soaked the carpet. I made to crawl towards him, but I was grabbed by the arm and hauled to my feet.

Debayo dragged me outside towards his car. If people heard the gunshot and my scream as I was dragged outside, they stayed in their rooms. Nobody was outside. And if they saw me being dragged off, they watched through their windows and turned away when I was dumped in the backseat of the car.

CHAPTER 16

DEBAYO HATED SLOPPINESS, but he *was* getting sloppier by the day. It had started with Ben, and now, he was unintentionally leaving trails of blunder after blunder—trails that were drawing the investigator called Jude close to him like blood called to a shark.

From his investigations of the man, Jude wasn't a talker. Debayo was scared of dangerous-looking men who didn't talk much, and it was why he was starting to panic.

He had seen the most grotesque things under the sun and the earth but never panicked. He had done the most unthinkable things, but he never flinched while doing them; that was the crux of his power in people's eyes. But this time round, the predator was terrified of being hunted, because Jude knew Debayo would go after Assad.

He was lucky Ben finished the job in other ways.

Smart man, though stupid for the messy job with Assad. All his men were trained to embrace their deaths if push came to shove. Nobody could know who he was. After Ben, there were two more botched jobs. Two more attempts at putting that silly fiancé in the ground. The love-struck man was proving hard to kill.

During the second attempt, his man had been a buffoon. He was gloating, telling Jude to stop protecting Assad, seeing as his woman was about to get married. The oaf even mentioned Debayo's name, but that was as far as he could get.

He seemed to have remembered to kill himself in place of Assad if things went awry and did that. The third was better. Good man, he didn't step out of his car when Jude ordered him to, and he fired at a police officer. Before Jude could stop the other officers, they rained bullets through him.

Debayo could blame his men all day and punish them, but he could also sense when the tide was shifting against him. Someone might call it the will of God, but he didn't believe in God, so he laid the blame for these mistakes on himself.

Now, the only thing the sure-footed investigator needed was a location. Not that Debayo would sit and wait for a bunch of cowards dressed in uniforms led by a dangerous man to come and get him.

He would do the job himself—there were vials of poison hidden in his office for such an emergency. He wouldn't forget everyone in his service, either. He'd pull them into the earth with him. He had to protect his friends, too. Or even in death, they would find ways to kill him again.

He wanted so badly to do away with the girl's fiancé, but he would be an idiot to attempt a fourth. For the first time in years, he wasn't sure what to do next, and he could feel the unrest coming from his men even while in Morocco.

Debayo was itching to go home—things would be better if he did. And if he couldn't try again with the fiancé, he would go for Jude's head. Nobody got to frighten him. And certainly not some puny investigator.

He called T-Bone. He had initially wanted to send him on the assignments, but he had some reservations. T-Bone was his right-hand man, and even though there wasn't a soul he trusted and relied on fully, he found he couldn't let him go. The damage would be worse if it were T-Bone in a situation against Jude.

And he was right. T-Bone would put up a fight before killing himself, but there was a chance he would still be gone. Debayo couldn't risk it and found that he was disgusted with himself for being so dependent on the man.

T-Bone answered. Debayo skipped the pleasantries and went straight to the point, like always.

"I'll be returning home soon. Tell the boys. I need to rein things in before they get out of hand." Things were already out of hand. He knew it was probably the same thought going through T-Bone's mind. But he had to maintain an air of defiance and control.

"Got it, sir. Should I send someone else? Someone better?"

"No," he said too hurriedly and too strongly. He paused and continued. "We can't risk it. You said yourself that he is already starting to snoop around. This will end soon when I'm there."

"Yes, sir. What about the girl?"

"What about her?" He paused again, realization shadowing his face. "You idiot! You think I brought her to kill her?"

"I only thought...well, things are not so good lately."

"She's not going to die. Do you hear me?" The sharpness of his tone surprised him. He wasn't used to getting riled up so easily.

"Got it, boss."

"We're getting married as soon as I land. I'll send word to her family, and they can move on from thinking any harm has come to her. Maybe we'll tell that boy she was supposed to get married to, too, if we can't kill him." His pessimism surprised him. Again.

"Wouldn't they try to find her if you reach out?" There was uncertainty in T-Bone's voice.

"Have you always been this stupid? I wouldn't give away my identity. It'll be a note with only a message."

"Yes, sir."

"Now, prepare for my arrival. How are the girls?" He didn't care about their health at all. The question was an indirect way of asking how many were still alive. T-Bone understood this.

"Two died last week, sir."

"I don't like wasted investments. We'll ship them right after the wedding. That would be all. I'll call you the day I fly."

"Yes, sir."

Debayo rested his elbows on the oak desk and propped up his chin. He had come too far to lose. Whatever he wanted, he always got. He wouldn't allow the girl's family to rattle him with their investigator friend. That meant one thing was for certain: Jude had to go.

Debayo grew up with his mother in the run-down parts of Axim. He was born to Nigerian parents in Adamawa.

Their respective families didn't welcome the union, so his parents eloped to Ghana to start a new life. His father disappeared six months after he was born, leaving his mother to clean the houses of the rich to raise him.

She spent the remaining days of her life nursing the heartbreak from when his father left. When he turned sixteen, his mother died, and he was left to care for himself. He worked countless jobs—carpentry, masonry, painting, and shoe making. He stole in between jobs, and it was the thing he was best at.

He could pick locks like a professional, pick pockets and get away with it in the full glare of people, and burgle people under the shade of the inky night. He was never caught. Policemen looked for him, and he was right in front of them, but they couldn't see him.

Soon, he developed a love for education. The money he stole barely fulfilled his needs as a young man. He began to steal heavier amounts, using the money to buy books and befriending students in his city.

He taught himself English, arithmetic, and history. The world began to fascinate him, and his fascination grew into an itch that could just not be ignored. He learned the smell and shape of wealth and followed its trails.

Debayo joined gangs, each one more daring than the other. He soon joined a gang whose proxy leader was educated at the secondary level. The man was fearless, or so they thought until he surrendered to policemen on a mission with two other members. The next educated person, Debayo, had grown into a tall, staggering twenty-three-year-old man.

In charge, Debayo grew bored of the routine robberies. Breaking into a house and making the family who lived there kneel with their hands over their heads was getting tired and lame. He wanted something more, something that promised a greater thrill.

He thought of breaking into the Palace that was reputed to be the home of gold. The Palace belonged to an old family that governed the city before the advent of a white-man-style government. And even now, they still governed it, sort of.

The chief was known to be an arrogant old thwart. His entire family lived off their greed and their subjects' loyalty and misery. The chief was celebrating his seventy-seventh birthday, and from what Debayo knew, the repulsive man thrived on admiration and praise. Debayo knew he just had to attend the celebration.

He spent days retrieving information from the spies he sent to the market and areas surrounding the Palace. They all told him the same thing—he could infiltrate the Palace so long as he knew how to act like a rich, greedy man. And that was no problem for Debayo at all.

Wherever wealth called, he answered. The rich old

men were all thieves dressed in finery, but they were also a bunch of idiots.

The day of the celebration arrived, and Debayo dressed in attire befitting a rich, greedy man. A kaftan, an expensive-looking pair of shoes, and an air of gravitas—all purchased with stolen money.

He planted spies among the crowds and in the marketplace so they could communicate by winking and accidentally touching each other. They were to make a run for it the moment something went wrong.

He introduced himself to the men surrounding the chief as a businessman who traveled the world, had heard of the might and benevolence of the chief, and just had to witness the celebration of his life and greatness.

The buffoons believed him, and when it was time for the royal dinner, he was promptly introduced to the chief. The chief sat in his grand chair, face and body withering, and listened to Debayo sing praises he hadn't earned.

"O great chief! All my travels have, as of today, amounted to prodigious relevance because they have led me to the honor of being in your presence. People sing praises of you, and so I feel I'll beat my chest and pull at my hair if I don't do the same," he said, all the while making expressive faces.

The chief's eyes twinkled, and he rubbed his slightly jutting-out stubby chin in pleasure. He nodded and looked around the room, noting everyone who shared Debayo's sentiments.

Debayo took this as his cue to continue. The old fool was so gullible—Debayo only had to play his cards right to have him in his palm.

"You've grown in wisdom and mercy, but ask any young woman in this city, and they'll tell you just how desirable they find you. You're grandiose, o kind chief, and your people's hearts swell with gratitude."

Debayo's voice alternated between the high-pitched tone of a town crier and the strained, demure voice of one who was indebted to a powerful man. It worked. The chief stroked a sagging cheek, and his eyes shone, delighted.

"Mr...err..." the chief began.

"Esun," Debayo answered. He heard people murmur at his unusual name, but that only fueled his confidence.

"Mr. Esun, you're kind. Thank you for gracing this occasion. Now, let's celebrate as people of high minds and ambitions!" All the while he spoke, the chief eyed the two gold rings on Debayo's fingers.

There was a cheer, and they feasted deep into the night. After the feast, Debayo was given a room to rest in the Palace. He did a mental jump and proceeded to eulogize the chief once more for such hospitality.

Before Debayo retreated to his guest room, the chief spoke to him about gold. The chief, being the idiot he was, didn't attempt to know the intricacies of Debayo's said business. Rather, he wanted to show Debayo his personal gold collection in unspoken hopes that Debayo would want to do the same.

Debayo beamed. It was better than he anticipated. He wanted gold from the museum, but the chief was making things easier by showing him his personal collection. He had to maintain his composure so as not to blow his cover.

He knew what he had to do. He went on and on about his own collection of gold hidden in a safe in his mansion. The lie brought something alive within him, and his mouth watered from speaking about all that wealth. That was all the chief needed to hear. He promised to visit Debayo in his mansion not too long from that time.

What a fool, Debayo thought. He hated stupid people and people who talked too much, and the chief was both. His excitement almost gave way to disgust, and he was terrible at hiding his disgust for people and things. It didn't take long for his voice and face to take on condescending forms.

The chief led Debayo to his room and retired to his quarters. Debayo didn't sleep right away. He spent the entire night strategizing and devising a foolproof plan to rob the chief. He sent word to his boys outside the Palace and slept patiently, waiting for morning.

Debayo woke up in high spirits the next day—it was

the day of the looting. After the royal breakfast, right before the chief dragged Debayo to his treasure trove, he was alerted to a premeditated commotion outside that needed the chief's attention.

It was time. Debayo made a show of retreating to his room in wait for the chief with one of his boys, who was disguised as his assistant. It was the first time T-Bone worked closely with Debayo.

When they were sure they weren't being monitored or followed, they meandered their way through the Palace until they arrived at the hideout of the gold. Debayo approached the guard stationed in front of the heavy door —T-Bone stayed a few feet away as a lookout.

Debayo made to engage the grouchy guard in a conversation about women, asking him if he got to be with women at all, given the nature of his job. The guard only grunted and looked straight ahead. Debayo sighed—they always chose the hard way without even knowing.

He moved closer to the guard, who could now sense some foulness. The hilt of a dagger was cushioned against Debayo's palm, warm and begging to be held.

The guard's eyes shot to Debayo's hand nestled in the pockets of his kaftan, and his jaws tightened, every hair on his skin raised.

"Stop!" he yelled, hoping someone could hear him. The end was so close—he could taste the stench of death on his tongue. He made to draw his own dagger out of its sheath. If he was going to die, he might as well take this trespasser with him. He was too late, however. By the time his dagger was out of its sheath, Debayo's knife was lodged deep in his heart.

Debayo stepped away and wiped the scant blood away, painting his hand red on the wall. He preferred clean deaths to messy ones, but he hadn't had a choice with this one. He shot a pitiful look at the body, already growing ashen, and kicked open the door. He had figured the door wasn't locked when the chief had only pushed it the previous night. The old fool was so confident in the abilities of his cowardly guard that he didn't keep his treasure under lock and key.

He would've loved to revel in the way his body rejoiced at being in the presence of the gold if he had more time. Instead, he gathered as many rings and necklaces as he could and fled. He motioned to T-Bone, and they jumped over the lowest part of the wall at the remote corner of the Palace.

Debayo, taking the lion's share, shared his loot among himself and his boys. He told them he was disbanding the group and that they all needed to go their separate ways. T-Bone insisted on sticking by him, so they migrated together to the country's capital.

He recruited men to do his dirty jobs for him while he

traveled the continent and helped people out of their misery so that they were indebted to him with their lives. He was clever; he cleaned up every mess he made and frustrated every police and investigator in Ghana.

He traced his old father to a village in Umuahia—the man had returned to Nigeria after leaving his newborn son and partner—and traveled to Nigeria to find him after T-Bone kidnapped and beat up the wrong old man who fit the descriptions of Debayo's father.

It was on a particularly bright afternoon when Debayo walked into the tiny hut that was meant to be his father's. The hut was small and made of mud with a dirty grey curtain in lieu of a door that stood lonely in the middle of the compound, its roof made of what looked like dried palm branches.

In front of the hut lay a lean old man on a tattered straw mat. Debayo ordered T-Bone to stay in the car and got out, feeling the sun unleash all its fury onto the ground. The man, used to being alone, save for his twenty-five-year-old niece, who visited twice every day, stirred in his sleep the moment he felt someone's presence.

His niece had already come to take care of him and wouldn't come again until the sun set. He opened his eyes only halfway, eyeing Debayo's approach. He tried to sit up against the hut wall, wheezing as he did so. His chest and ribs moved laboriously with every intake and expulsion of breath.

Debayo stood in front of the old man and then sat on his haunches, watching the man as the man watched him. Finally, Debayo smiled. It was him.

"Do you know who I am?" he asked.

"No...please...spare me," he said, pausing between words to breathe. Even he could see the murderous intent in Debayo's eyes. "I am a...nobody. A poor man...without a...family. With...no...money." He groaned, a feeble hand clutching his chest.

Debayo cocked his head. "You *chose* to be without a family. Look at me and tell me you do not know me. Come on. Open your eyes before I force them open."

The old man looked into Debayo's eyes for a moment before looking away into the distance. "Your eyes...were the...first things...I...noticed when...the...midwife told me... I could...go in...and see...my wife...and son. You...have... her...eyes."

Debayo smiled. "Good. I'm not going to bother asking you why you left. But you are going to pay for it."

The old man wheezed and sighed. "I...am...already... dead."

"Good." Debayo stood. "I will just help speed it along."

He motioned to T-Bone to join him. They carried the

man inside the hut, and Debayo pressed a pillow into his face with an expectant and hopeful look.

A few moments later, the old man stopped twitching.

In the next few months, Debayo mingled with men who smelled of filthy wealth and joined in their businesses—child trafficking, especially of girls. His first child trafficking gig was in Nigeria. He met and partnered with Mr. Goodwill, a veteran of the trade. They dispatched three cars to abduct forty girls in Maiduguri and Kano over the course of two weeks.

They kept the girls locked up in a warehouse in a remote part of Maiduguri for six days, feeding them badly cooked rice. On the seventh day, a truck carried them to the airport in the middle of the night, where they were transferred onto Debayo's private plane. The girls were flown into Ghana and Sierra Leone, where they were sold to the highest bidders. For the next five years, he continued trafficking girls, expanding his reach to Rwanda, Senegal, Kenya, South Africa, and Congo. With money overflowing his bank accounts, Debayo built houses across Ghana and invested in normal businesses, too; it was important to keep up with appearances.

The next thing he did was get married. She was a

beautiful one with a lithe body and wide, innocent eyes. She bore him a daughter, the one thing he truly loved in the world—even more than himself or his wealth. She was sent away to study and live in Canada when she came of age.

His daughter didn't know who her father was or what truly happened to her mother. As far as she knew, her mother died after battling an illness that her father didn't want to discuss because he was still grieving.

Debayo stabbed his wife after she found the girls in the basement. She threatened to inform the police and then placed a call to them. He clicked his tongue against his teeth as he shook his head at her folly before burying a knife in her belly. He escaped and relocated with the girls and his workers under cover of the night to his current mansion, serving as his home for the past decade.

It was a magnificent building made of concrete, nestled at the edge of Elubo with high walls and courtyards five hundred meters in length separating the house from the gates. It looked out of place next to a small, poor town filled with small brick and mortar houses. To everyone on the outside, the mansion looked proud and felt alive, watching you as you passed. To some on the inside, even the magnificence of the mansion could not do away with the feeling of being trapped: an airy prison—a place where you had to hide within yourself to survive.

Debayo called his daughter every day and flew to Canada to be with her when he was able, though it was rare. If he were ever captured or made the mistake of ratting his business partners out to the Bureau of National Investigations, which had been looking for them for years, his little girl would sleep and not wake up to her perfect life anymore.

Ever since he had chanced upon Asiya, he found that she was gradually becoming the other person he loved apart from himself and his daughter. She would be his second chance at romance and marriage, her purity absolving him from the horror he was. If he could love and keep someone so beautiful and pure, maybe the disgust that crept up on him each time he thought about his life would leave him alone. That, and the fact that the sight of her could get his pants twitching. She was going to love him back, and they were going to be perfectly happy. He was going to make sure she didn't ever find out that he was a monster, and his daughter would love her, too.

The girl's family could go hang—her fiancé too. He was going to create another life for himself and live, truly, this time.

I'M IN BED, watching the ceiling. A bit of my hair falls into my eyes as I check the clock on the wall and huff. I haven't really spoken to Lila today. She brought my breakfast and told me she'll be back so we can talk.

She looked and sounded different this morning, like something was bothering her. Right when I'm wondering what's wrong, I hear the usual two raps on the door. Speak of the devil. I rush to the door to open it for her. It was her idea to lock it when she wasn't with me—one of her many expert pieces of advice.

I open the door to find Lila's adorable face and stand aside for her to enter before I shut the door. She slumps onto my bed and unwraps her turban before facing me. "How are you?"

She hasn't asked me this in a while. Our relationship has evolved beyond me telling her my thoughts and feelings only after she asks me, so it causes me to back up a little.

"I'm...okay, I guess. You?"

"No...How are you? Really?"

I slump beside her on the bed and think about her question. While I'm slowly accepting my fate, I miss my family and Assad terribly. Sometimes, when she leaves me alone here to retire to her room, I stay up crying into the bedding. I only fall asleep when my eyes decide they cannot produce any more tears and my thoughts exhaust me. So, no. I'm not okay.

"I'm tired," I say. It's not far from the truth. I *am* tired.

"Just that?" She looks directly at me, and I feel a tad bit uncomfortable. She's trying to tread into uncharted territory. She wants to hold the two halves of my body apart, baring my insides to all her senses.

I sigh. Let's do it, then. "I miss my family. I miss Father's hearty laugh, baritone voice, and Mother's...well, everything that makes her Mother. I miss Aisha and Zainab. Those girls drive me mad sometimes, but now, looking back, I wouldn't have it any other way. I miss my old life...I miss school. I miss Assad."

She perks up at his name, and I snort. She looks like a child eager to get a reward. So, I give it to her.

"I keep wishing we'd been married already. I miss walking around with him, discussing almost everything under the sun. I miss stealthily watching his lips."

"Astaghfirullah!" she says, and our faces erupt with grins. "Keep it halal, sis. Rein in your thoughts...stops thinking about his lips."

"Amongst other things," I continue. I can feel my cheeks warming up.

"*Other things?*" Her voice is playful and light.

"*Other things,*" I say, and we clutch our bellies as another bout of laughter takes hold of us. I grow somber once more and say, "But all that's gone now."

"It doesn't have to be," she says. She smiles and reaches over to hold my hand.

I know it's all over now, and I don't understand what she means by what she said, but I nod and try to allow her positivity to wash over me.

"I'm sorry. About everything that has happened to you." She looks so sincere that I melt inside.

I roll my eyes and smile. "Since when did you become this dramatic?" Now, it's her turn to chuckle. "You don't have to be sorry. I met you, remember?"

She nods, and I squeeze her hand in mine. "How are you?" I return the intense gaze she shot me earlier.

She averts her eyes and looks like she's thinking about it too. Her eyes look back at me, and a sad smile plays on her lips. "I miss my parents too. And I wish I could think or even hope of seeing them again. But now, all I can wish for is that they were still alive."

I do a sharp intake of breath, and I'm sure she heard it because she waves the worry on my face away. I hold her hand tighter, unsure of what to say. She lost her parents; how terrible. She looks like she still has a lot to say.

"Mami died from cancer, and he killed Baba. Right in front of me. The monster." Her voice takes on a sharpness I've never heard before. "Then he brought me here to remind me that he could end my life too if he so wished. God, I hate him."

"I'm sorry," I say without thinking.

"For what?" The smile on her lips is completely at odds with her shimmering eyes. "I met you, remember?"

We chortle, but I ache inside. How is she able to live like she didn't witness a tragedy? I suddenly feel angst and overwhelming sadness, and I realize that Lila is my one true friend.

She's not the type of friend life has thrown at me because we happened to be in the same space over the years. I truly care for her and am determined to hold on to her. It's hard to bring myself to say it, but in case I never see my family or Assad again, I know she'll be there to hold the space that's slowly widening in my chest.

"But we may have a shot at this." She brings me out of my reverie.

"At what?" I ask.

"We may have a chance at getting out of here." Her face and voice are impassive; it's hard to read them.

I scramble up and rush to the door, opening it and closing it again when I'm satisfied nobody is listening in on us. "You do realize someone could've been listening, right? And what do you mean? Don't joke with me," I say all in one breath.

"I'm not joking." She sits up. "I've thought of a plan, and Zayn is going to help us."

I croon at the mention of Zayn, and she looks away in an attempt to hide her growing smile. Boy, is she smitten.

"Asiya, you can do that later," she says when it looks like she has a grip on her emotions.

"Okay, fine. Talk to me. How on earth do you suggest leaving this place right under everyone's nose?" I walk back towards her and sit cross-legged on the floor in front of her.

"Who said anything about escaping under someone's nose?" She sounds smug. That's new. She grins at the confusion on my face, and we plan everything to detail the day before Debayo's return.

He's set to arrive today at sunset. Despite knowing it's probably never going to happen, I wish he's killed in an accident on his way here so that we don't have to do any of this. I don't know what his death would mean for Lila and me while we're still here, but it doesn't hurt to dream.

We laugh a lot and talk like nothing unusual is happening, but when she walks out, I grapple with a whole gamut of emotions. It's as though equal amounts of sorrow, helplessness, and fear have been thrown in my face.

Just a while before sunset, I pray asr and put on a black dress I found in the closet. I tie my hair in a ponytail with a scrunchie, wrap a red hijab around my head, and slip my feet into black flats. I check my reflection in the mirror, taking in my sunken eyes and prominent weight loss.

I looked away, not having the strength to look too closely. Despite my efforts to eat properly—well, I mean Lila's efforts, mostly—I've failed at maintaining my original weight. It's hard when you have to pretend your life isn't going downhill. It gets harder to mute all the noise in your head that's enough to swallow you whole, even if you met an amazing human being in the midst of this accursed mansion.

A sharp knock startles me. It isn't the sound of Lila's knock. I take a deep breath and walk five long strides to the door. I open it, revealing the face and lean body of a guard. I step out, close the door gently behind me, and take the lead. I silently reject his offer to help me descend the stairs to reach the courtyard and join the other workers in waiting. I look around, and my eyes finally find whom they are looking for. Lila winks, and her eyes flitter to someone—or something—else. I can't tell from where I stand.

No sooner had I gotten here than the massive gates open, and a black Rolls Royce speeds into the compound. A guard rushes to open the car door, and Debayo gets down, his piercing eyes finding me the moment he's out of the car.

I hold his gaze for a moment and avert my eyes, looking at the rhythmic swaying shadows of the palm trees. He walks forward, approaching me directly—it takes everything in me to keep standing without moving an inch. He stops to stand before me, smiling. I fight the urge to jump on him and claw his eyes out.

"My dear! How I have missed you."

Who says 'dear' anymore? I look at him with pure and unmasked loathing as he reaches for my hand and bends over to kiss it. He lifts his head, smiling some more, and then takes in my appearance. His eyes linger where the dress hugs my hips, and when he raises his head, his face has contorted into a frown.

"Lila!" he bellows.

I panic at the sound, my heart thudding in my chest. My palms grow sweaty, and my eyes dart everywhere in search of Lila—I don't find her where I found her earlier. She appears before him, her head slightly bowed. I can sense her trepidation, and I wonder if anyone can feel it too.

"You have not done as I asked."

She lifts her head, a thin line of sweat snaking down her neck. Done as he asked? What's going on? My legs wobble, and I struggle to keep them steady.

"I asked you to feed her well and make sure she grows some flesh, but all I can see is evidence of how skinny she has grown the past few weeks."

A tiny part of me is relieved, and the rest is groaning on the inside because this is my fault. I remember all the times she was on me to eat with worry etched on her face. I wish I could kick myself for being so dumb. How did I not see that I was giving him a chance to hurt her?

He orders a guard to lock Lila up in a room on the third floor. She doesn't put up a fight, nor does she look at me. Oh, God. This can't be happening. All our plans to get out of here...

I remain in the courtyard well after almost everyone has dispersed. When I'm alone with him, save for a few guards, I look him square in the face and plead on Lila's behalf. I tell him it's my fault; I add that Lila is the only friend I've made, and if he truly cares for me, he should free her. Using that last bit makes me want to throw up in his face—if he cares for me. Like hell he does.

As I speak, he looks at me as though searching for something in my face. I hope my desperation isn't obvious, and even if it were, he wouldn't guess that I had any other motive for pleading for Lila's freedom.

After a moment, he nods at the guard who sent her upstairs and goes to get her. I thank him, flashing a smile that's at odds with my cold eyes, and turn to go up to my room. He mentions my name just as I begin to ascend the stairs.

I stop in my tracks, and a few heartbeats later, I spin around to listen to what he has to say. He rubs his smooth and jeweled hands together, like a child about to announce that he scored good grades in his examinations.

"My dear," he begins excitedly, searching my face once more for something. I don't know what, but I've made up my mind not to betray my intentions regarding him. "We will finally be married next month, and trust that it will be legal. Meanwhile, we will spend time together and get acquainted," he said, sounding pleased with himself.

I remain silent, praying we're able to get out of this place tomorrow, In Shaa Allah. I cannot, for the life of me, imagine being married to this man. I would rather die.

"See you at breakfast tomorrow, dear."

I take this as my cue to retreat to my room.

The next morning, the day of our planned escape, Lila brings my breakfast up to my room as usual, and I endeavor to eat every bite as a silent apology for the previous night. She doesn't seem affected by what happened, even though I catch her attempts to conceal her smiles at my effort to eat everything on the serving tray.

We don't talk about the escape.

An hour after she leaves my room, she returns to inform me that Debayo has requested my presence at the table. She winks to signal that she has already plopped drops of liquid ecstasy in his morning tea. My anxiety calms a bit—no challenges so far. The other workers can also be counted on not to go close to the dining area while the boss has his meal. She then heads to other parts of the mansion, where she will summon all the guards on duty to their quarters, saying that the boss is going to join them shortly and make an announcement.

It's a lie, of course.

The halls of the mansion are large and painted mostly white with antique décor. The dining room is no exception. It's large enough to hold a feast with an insanely expensive-looking dining table and twelve chairs around it—yes, I have counted. And again, they're antiques. I sit beside him as he had requested and wait expectantly for him to start eating, but he doesn't touch the food. He stares at me, and I look at the wall clock above his head. Sweat starts gathering at the back of my neck. I wipe my wet hands on my jeans. What the hell is going on? Why isn't he eating?

"I'm sure you don't like your tea cold," I say.

"In a hurry to leave my presence? Am I that insufferable?"

I scoff without meaning to and cover my mouth. This guy is a psychopath—the littlest thing could tick him off. We're so close to completing our plan, I'd be an idiot to blow it up. He *is* insufferable, but I suppose I'll tolerate him just a little while longer.

As long as he drinks that tea.

"I guess I am. You look like you'd rather die than sit here with me," he purrs the words like a contented cat. He smiles, still staring at me.

God, what I'd give to make him lose that stupid smile. At least he's honest with himself.

"Why?" I hear myself asking. I purse my lips, but it's too late. He heard me.

"Why what?"

I want more than anything to roll my eyes at this very moment. Stupid questions are the worst. He knows what I mean, but look at him gaslighting me. I glare at him and say nothing. Any niceness I had in store to help me tolerate him is out the window.

He chuckles. "I'll tell you one day. For now, I just want you to be happy so we can get to know each other."

This time, I roll my eyes. "Yeah, right."

That bloody smile appears on his face again. "Honest."

"I don't think you know what that word means," I snap. I'm treading a dangerous path, but I don't care. "I hate you, you know."

He doesn't look surprised or at all affected by what I just said, and it makes me angrier. "I know. It's all over your face. But some of the best marriages are built on hatred. Do you know what holds it together? Faith. That one day, you'd wake up and not want to strangle the other person."

"Oh, I doubt that." I think I should just shut up and let him drink the tea.

"I love you, Asiya. I admit this is...wrong, but it's all I have. All I've always had to do to get what I want. I don't know anything else."

I stay silent and look away.

"Maybe one day, you'll look past the monster you think I am." He says the words softly as if he believes them. As if being a murderer was something I could look over like one might for an odd laugh.

Now, I have to say something. "You *are* a monster. I don't just think it. It's a fact. And I'm sure everyone here knows it, too. They're just too chicken to say it or even imply it. I'd like to go up and rest, please, if you don't want to have your breakfast anymore." I don't know what I'm thinking by saying this, but I hope he drinks the damn tea.

Instead, he gets up and stretches his right hand toward me. I can feel my face contort in confusion. Huh? What does he think he's doing? What about the tea?

I must look horrified because he takes my hand in his and says, "You look like you could pass out. It's just tea. I'll have something else if it's too cold by the time we return."

Return? From where? Oh, my God. This is all going down the drain. Lila...

He tugs on my hand as he walks out of the dining room and in the direction of a locked door adjacent to it. I am sweating, and my heart is about to jump out of my chest. I keep turning my head, casting worried glances in the direction of the dining room. He lets go of my hand and turns the key in the lock, opening the door. We step in, and the air rushes out of my lungs.

It's a library, a huge one at that, and it's absolutely gorgeous. There are books—so many I could never finish counting them—arranged on lacquer shelves, and three rolling ladders are leaning against them for me to whisk through them all. I'm almost tempted to let myself go and revel in this heaven on earth, this fairytale dream, but our plan is about to be blown if he doesn't drink that tea. I realize he is staring at me, waiting for me to say something. Here goes nothing.

"This place is amazing," I say, making a show of turning my head in every direction. I look back at him and smile my fakest smile. He takes it well, looking pleased with himself. I hope this means my plan is working. "Thank you," I add, walking to the closest shelf to trace my fingers along the spine of a book. *Anthills of the Savannah.* Chinua Achebe. Interesting. I keep my eyes on that shelf and see names I'm familiar with and admire: Ama Ata Aidoo, Buchi Emecheta, Mariama Bâ, Ngũgĩ wa Thiong'o, and Nawal El Saadawi.

As if reading my mind, he says, "I looked into what you like to read. I hope I got it right?" His question is left hanging, like he wants confirmation that he has pleased me. Well, I might as well use that to my advantage.

I look at him and flash yet another fake smile, nodding my head. 'Looked into'? Great way to say stalked. Suddenly, I am terrified, and I turn away to face the bookshelf again so he can't see it on my face. How long did he watch me? What else does he know about me? Did he watch my family too? *Focus, Asiya,* I think. Now, my priority is getting out of here. I'll think about these things later.

I feel him standing behind me. I turn and take his right hand in my hands, smiling. It is not a genuine smile. I need to do something to get him back into the dining room.

"I appreciate this gesture. But I—"

"Please, don't say you don't like it. This is me trying to make you happy. I meant it when I said I loved you. Accept this. In addition, I'll do whatever you want me to do—that does not involve leaving my house—and spend as much time with you as possible."

I give his hand a squeeze and let go. "I was about to ask you to have your breakfast. I don't want you to walk around with an empty stomach."

He grins and turns to walk in the direction of the door. I am still standing in the same spot, my heart racing. He pauses before opening the door.

"You can stay here. You don't have to sit with me while I eat. Well, that is if you don't mind." He scratches his hair and glances at the floor or his slippers before looking back up at me. It's the perfect opportunity.

"I don't mind," I say, walking towards him. I need to make sure he drinks that tea.

He grins again, opening the door for me. He waits for me to walk out of the library before hurrying in front of me again to open the door to the dining room for me. I am amused—he has a jump in his step.

He sits in his chair and lifts the mug. He sniffs it. "It's cold, but I don't mind. Anything to make you happy."

I smile—a genuine smile this time—and wait. I don't have to wait for long. He brings the mug to his lips, but before he takes a sip, he pauses again. "I took a gamble. We weren't sure you'd be the one to open the gates."

Somehow—and I feel sick for this—I feel sorry for him, knowing what's to come. He takes a sip and shudders before doubling over the table. The mug hits the carpeted floor, and rest of the tea soaks the carpet. He slips off the edge of the table and falls on the floor, unconscious.

I wait a few seconds just to make sure and then stand and walk over to him, slipping my right hand into his breast pocket to feel for the key. I draw it out and head for his bedroom.

Lila is supposed to lock the guards in their quarters and meet me in his bedroom so that we can look for the safe together. I stall when I'm close to his bedroom, deciding to wait for Lila by the heavy door.

Minutes pass, and I begin to grow uneasy. There's this unshakeable feeling that something is wrong. Lila is late, and my inhibitions tell me there's trouble. I hear footsteps —heavy footsteps—and I freeze at the shadow of a man coming around the corner.

My eyes bounce around the corridor, looking for a place to hide. I find none. I'm suddenly scared Lila hadn't been able to lock the guards up, or worse, she's been captured. And here I am, a silly girl doing what could endanger her and her family ten times.

"What are you doing here?" a voice booms.

I spin around to face T-Bone. This is the second time I have come face to face with him, and I'd rather Debayo himself woke up than deal with this...creep. I haven't forgotten when I witnessed the murder of a woman at his hand some time ago. I know he'd kill me with his bare hands if I give him a reason to, so I try to ignore his leering and put on a nonchalant demeanor.

"My husband-to-be has sent me here to get him something from his bedroom," I lie, placing too much emphasis on *husband-to-be*. Makes me sick to say it, but a girl's got to do what a girl's got to do.

"You? Why would he do that? He doesn't even send me, his most trusted guard, up here."

"Well, I am to be his wife. Why wouldn't he?" I say, sounding bolder than I intended, and then cock my head to one side. "And what are *you* doing here?"

"I heard *your* footsteps," he says, smirking. He then squints at me as if deciding whether to believe me.

We're running out of time. Someone is bound to discover Debayo any minute now, though I had locked the door to the dining area. And things will definitely get worse the moment Lila arrives at this scene. I'm scared of what's happened to her, but I also wish she'd stay wherever she is.

I'm beginning to lose the air of confidence that would influence his decision to believe me. As if things are not going untoward enough already, he spots the key in my hand. He seizes me by the arm, sandwiching me between him and the wall.

"What are you doing with that key, and where is the boss?" he hisses, flecks of his saliva dripping onto my face. He's being loud, too loud.

I close my eyes, tears pricking and streaming down my face. This is the end. *I'm sorry, Lila—*

In an instant, his grip on my arm relaxes. I open my eyes to find him sprawled on the floor, the white carpet turning crimson. Lila stands there, a broken pot of roses in her hand. Her chest is heaving, and she looks petrified.

"He didn't hear me come up behind him...he was too focused on you. He was returning from an errand. That's why he is still around. I've locked up the rest."

I look from the guard lying unconscious in a pool of his blood to Lila's panic-stricken face and back to the guard.

"I had to do something," she says, looking at him too. Would you rather we were found out? He would've killed us both without his boss's permission."

I notice how she says *his boss*. This is truly happening. We're going to be free.

"Besides, I don't think he'll die. If the authorities get here on time, he'll live. We don't have much time. Let's do it," she says, gesturing towards the door. We rush toward it, and I turn the handle. The door opens, startling us. We hadn't expected this.

Nevertheless, we enter the room, searching everywhere for a safe. This room, unlike the others, has black a black interior and décor. The bedding looks like no one has slept on it in months. There is a small shelf with books, which surprises me. I didn't peg Debayo for a reader; I assumed he stocked the library for me. I'd check them out, but this is not the time. I look in his closet and find it. It's black and has a keyhole and a handle. I motion to Lila, who's looking behind a beautiful bookcase.

She joins me and watches while I insert the key and turn it. There's a click, and the door opens. What we see next discourages us. The actual safe is built into the wall, and to open it, one has to input a code. We stand there for a while, trying to guess what the code could be.

I suggest using his birthdate, but we both have no idea what it is, so Lila goes through his documents. She finds his birth year after ransacking the drawers in the room, and I punch it in. The safe doesn't open. We try two random years—his mother's birth year—which we found in his documents, and my birth year.

With every incorrect passcode, my heart trembles

worse. We have only one attempt left before the safe locks us out completely. We stand there for about half an hour, not knowing what to do next.

Lila has slumped onto the floor by the safe, looking defeated. I take a look around, searching for places she might have forgotten. I open his wardrobe, and the strong scent of perfume almost knocks me off my feet. I rummage through his clothes and find an envelope wedged between two kaftans.

I tear it open and take out the documents in it, scanning them briefly. There are two birth certificates and one death certificate, coupled with several travel documents with his name and another name—Tomi.

"No way," I mutter, my mouth hanging open.

"What?" Lila asks, pushing herself up and toward me.

"He's been married before. And he has a daughter. I think she's called Tomi."

"You're kidding, right?" Lila echoes. She's just as bewildered as I am, if not more.

"Wish I were," I whisper.

I hand her the documents and dig into the envelope once more, pulling out three pictures. The first one is of him, a petite lady with an immaculate face and a girl who looks about five years old. He looks...genuinely happy with the girl balanced on his lap. The other two are of the girl, one photo of her in her teens and another of her possibly in her twenties. Wow. She's gorgeous. And somehow, I feel sorry for her for having Debayo as a father.

"Let's try this," Lila says, and I almost jump. I've been staring too long at the pictures, my mind running wild. I nod, watching her walk back to the safe with a document in her hand.

"Which one is that?" I ask.

"Tomi's birth certificate. I saw the pictures...I have a feeling he loves her like crazy. It makes sense to use hers. And you're staring too much."

I realize I'm clutching the pictures now, and I drop them atop the other documents. "I know, right? It's just...it feels surreal for him to have a daughter. And she looks so innocent and untainted by his filth. I'm not entirely surprised he's been married before, but this?" My voice trails off at the mental image of Tomi's mother. "And how do you think she died?"

Lila shrugs. "No idea. I just hope she wasn't murdered. But I wouldn't put it past him."

I feel cold when her words hit me, and I cradle my body in my arms. God, I hope she found peace in death, however she died.

Lila gasps, and I look in her direction. The safe is open, but we can't celebrate our little success just yet. If anyone frees up the guards, we're done for.

We dump the documents and some money we've

found in the safe in a tote bag Lila brought with her and speed down the stairs to the basement. Lila picks the lock on the door and turns the handle.

We don't wait to see the girls come out, because on the way here, we heard the guards beginning to kick on the door to the quarters they'd been locked in, and it's just a matter of time before someone tries to find out what is happening.

We get out of the house, and Lila locks the house from the outside with the keys and padlock she'd stolen earlier. We'd wanted to wait until every one of the girls left first, but we've run out of time, and we think the investigators would want to question them.

Lila takes the documents and uses a stick to dig them in a hole while I stand watch. I see a car approach us, and I tap Lila on the shoulder. She sees it, too, and smiles. When the confusion on my face doesn't wane, she mouths, "Zayn."

He stops the car, and Lila gets in beside him while I sit in the back.

"Salaam alaikum," he says, looking over his shoulder at me with a shy smile. Nice to finally meet you, Asiya."

"Wa alaikum salaam. And likewise," I respond, feeling some sense of calm as I settle into the backseat.

Zayn calls the BNI on his phone and passes it to Lila.

She tells them everything she thinks they should know before hanging up, including the documents she'd hidden.

He drives in the direction of what I assume is Greater Accra. I had previously persuaded Lila to stay with my family if our plans to escape succeeded. She wasn't sure if my family would want her at first, but I convinced her. I'm sure everyone would love her.

I throw my head back, placing it on the headrest and drawing a heavy breath. My eyes are moist. I never thought I'd see this day. I'm going home—no, *we're going home.*

CHAPTER 18

AFTER ABOUT SIX hours on the road, Asiya recognized the traffic slowly building up in Tesano. She exhaled sharply, to which Lila looked back at her, eyebrows raised.

"We're here," Asiya said, voice small and throat parched.

"Right. Just tell me the way to go," Zayn intoned. It was the second time he had spoken since they left Debayo's mansion. The first was when he asked them if they'd like some water. They were too shaken and relieved to respond with words, and only shook their heads. He'd bought three bottles from a hawker anyway, but only Lila had taken a sip of hers. The rest of the six hours had been filled with culpable silence.

Asiya's head lay on the headrest, the bottle of water gradually growing warmer on her lap. Her head had stayed in that position for what seemed like eons, her gaze on the passing scenery until she recognized her town. She sat up with a bolt, her eyes misting as she clutched the bottle of water.

Lila reached behind to squeeze her hand and smile. Her own eyes were shimmering, both from the fact that her old life was lost forever and also that she was in that car with people she'd come to care for deeply. Her thoughts had been all over the place during the journey, her mind playing the reality she'd lived for the past five years in a loop. It always started with the time her mother fell ill, to when her father had the misfortune to encounter Debayo, to her parents' death, her abduction and servitude, and finally, Asiya.

Whenever her mind arrived at her meeting and friendship with Asiya, the ache would dull a little, and she'd feel lighter than she had only a few seconds before. Her tussling with both her past and future wasn't as rigorous as they neared Asiya's home; the uncertainty no longer loomed like a haunted building in the middle of nowhere.

"There!" Asiya said, pointing to a white building with walls turning brown from the dust. The gates surrounding it that had once been opened to steal her away now greeted her return.

Zayn parked directly in front of the building, and in

the minutes that followed, nobody moved a muscle or said a word.

"You shouldn't keep your family waiting," Zayn said, a broad smile plastered on his face. "Even if they're not expecting you—*especially* if they're not expecting you."

"Thank you. Both of you," she whispered. A lone tear made its way steadily down her right cheek as she looked from Lila to Zayn to Lila again.

"I'd do it all over again," Zayn professed.

Asiya wanted more than anything to leave the car and see her family again. They were so close—closer than they'd been for the past nightmarish weeks. Yet, her body wouldn't move. She felt a sadness she couldn't make sense of, wondering how her family was faring and if they thought she wasn't alive at all.

Zayn and Lila exchanged a worried look after they realized Asiya was still in the car, but before Lila could say a word, another car came to a halt behind them. All three exchanged looks this time around, fear on their faces. Something felt off. The Range Rover looked too familiar.

Lila and Asiya got out of the car just in time to see a fuming Debayo exiting his car. Their mouths dropped open as they watched him approach them with slightly sluggish steps.

"What's the matter? Were you not expecting to see me? I haven't driven myself in years. But you!" He pointed to Asiya and Lila, stopping just short of a few feet away from them. "You just made me do it. Like I said earlier, I'd do anything for you." He dropped his hand and gazed at Asiya. "I thought you were gradually coming around, feeling something for me too. Smart girl."

Lila looked at Asiya, wide-eyed and confused.

"I'll explain later," she mouthed.

"We could build a life together, Asiya. You and me. You could have anything you want in the world. All you have to do is ask." He swept an arm in the direction of his car, and it nearly made him stumble.

Zayn exited the car now, joining Lila and Asiya. Debayo grinned and pulled a gun from the inner pocket of his vest. He aimed the gun at them, and it shook from the tremor in his hand.

"Make one move toward those gates," he said, gesturing to the gates with the gun, then chuckled "I don't have to tell you what will happen, do I?"

Lila clutched Asiya's hand, and Zayn moved to stand between them and Debayo.

"You," he said, pointing the gun at Zayn. "You are going to regret getting involved. It is obvious who among the two is your girlfriend, and she is going back with me. Asiya wouldn't be interested in a low-life like you." He grinned at Lila, who now had tears in her eyes.

Zayn moved closer to Debayo, flexing his muscles. "No

one is going anywhere with you. And the only place *you* are going is jail."

Lila shared a terrified look with Asiya at his bold moves. "Zayn, he will kill you!"

"It doesn't hurt to try," Zayn muttered. He lunged forward and punched Debayo in the face.

Debayo took a few steps back, but smiled as he wiped the blood from the corner of his mouth. "Always the hard way."

He raised and fired his pistol at Zayn's left shoulder faster than any of them could blink.

Asiya broke free from Lila's grip, pounding at the gates, screaming for someone to help. No one opened them.

"No one home?" Debayo taunted. He looked at Zayn, who leaned against the Range Rover with a bloody hand clutching his shoulder.

Lila remained rooted in her spot, wringing her hands as tears fell down her cheeks.

"I can break your face with my bare hands, boy. But fortunately for you, I don't get my hands dirty anymore." Then he shot Zayn's left leg.

Lila screamed as Zayn slipped down onto the ground, groaning in pain. This time, she rushed to his aid and helped him to get back into his car, only to see Debayo grab Asiya's arm from the rearview window. Right then, the gates opened, revealing a bedraggled Harif. He took a step backward, his hand covering his mouth as his wide-open eyes took in the spectacle in front of him.

"Hello, Harif," Debayo drawled, grinning. But his smile faltered at the sight of two police cars driving closer, blocking Debayo's car. Zayn had called them before getting out of his car and getting into a fight with Debayo.

Five policemen approached Debayo, handguns raised. The one who looked like the senior policeman held up an ID. "Mr. Debayo Adelola, you are under arrest. Drop your weapon, let the girl go, and put your hands up!"

Debayo looked around at their faces—Harif, Lila, and then at the policeman who shouted the order. He took a long look at Asiya, let her go, and raised his hands, dropping the gun into the dirt. A policeman wearing gloves rushed to retrieve the pistol and dropped it into a plastic bag. At the same time, another rushed forward to cuff Debayo's hands.

Asiya inched closer to Harif, her face wet and the edges of her lips up in a wide smile.

"How...where...how?" Harif began. His brain could no longer form coherent questions in that space of time.

"It's a long story. And there's someone I'd like you to meet." Asiya looked back at Lila, and she paused before getting out of the car. "My friend, Lila. She helped me escape, and she's lost her family. I want her to stay with us."

Lila smiled what she hoped was a normal smile, but

whipped around when she heard a car start to drive away. Asiya called out to Zayn as she did, but he had pulled himself into the driver's seat and looked at them once before looking straight ahead and driving away. Lila started to run after him, then stopped when she realized he might not want her to. For the next few months, she would continue to wonder if he kept the car engine idling until she stepped out because he'd wanted to leave without saying goodbye.

Lila was crying now, and Asiya held her hand as Harif looked on, still in shock. The lead policeman invited the girls to one of the police cars to give a statement. Harif joined them, tearing up as they narrated their ordeal.

Afterward, they went inside the house. Harif shut the gate and walked ahead to inform the remainder of his family that they were whole again.

Plus, an additional member.

On their way to the living room, Asiya drew Lila close to her. "How was he able to wake up?" she asked. The question was directed at herself, but Lila answered anyway.

"Did he drink it cold?"

"Yes. He kept stalling like he knew there was something in the tea."

"Whether he knew or not, the poison loses its potency if the drink is cold," Lila said, her voice weary.

Asiya was not convinced. "I think he knew," she mused. "So, he intentionally waited for it to grow cold so he could follow us here."

"Asiya," Lila sighed, "whatever the case may be, the police have him now. We are safe. That is all that matters."

"I suppose," Asiya said, drawing in a deep breath. It was all over now. She was going to see her family again— well, the rest of her family.

Harif walked into the living room where his wife and two other daughters were huddled. Aisha was talking and gesticulating wildly with her hands about something she had seen on TV while Zainab looked on, attentive, with an amused smile on her lips.

"You took a while at the gate. Who was it?" Ameera said. Despite the illusion of normalcy, her episodes had become more frequent, and dark circles surrounded her eyes.

"Asiya," Harif said as Asiya entered the room, followed by Lila.

Aisha and Zainab squealed, springing up from their places on the floor. Zainab jumped, wrapping her little arms around Asiya's neck, while Aisha held on to Asiya's hand a little too painfully. Ameera sat there, stunned. She had envisioned this moment many times, imagining that she'd be the first to fling her arms around her daughter.

She'd imagined that she'd cry and laugh all at the same time.

She allowed her daughters to hug and fuss over Asiya even when she wanted to because she didn't have the heart to deprive the girls of their joy, the joy of touching their sister and realizing she was real flesh and blood.

The other reason was when Asiya walked in with the stranger, something had shifted in her. Her heart had slowed with its burning, and she'd felt at peace for the first time in a long time. Her head had cleared at that moment, and she felt new. Untainted. Free. The things she was anchored to let go of their grip on her. And so, it was worth it to sit back and watch her—them.

"Aisha, it hurts," Asiya said.

"Sannu," Aisha chuckled, eyes shimmering in addition to her apology. "I just don't want you to leave again."

After the girls settled into a couch, everyone except Asiya and Harif turned to look at Lila. She felt their stared burn her skin. Not because they were unfriendly—they were querying and quizzical—and she hung her head a little bit. She wished the ground would open up to swallow her. She shuffled her feet, glancing at Asiya as she did.

"Right," Asiya said breezily with a smile. She felt like she was floating, and her heart threatened to burst out of her chest. "Everyone, meet Lila. We escaped together, and

I want her to join our family as she...erm...lost hers." The last part was a mere whisper.

Ameera exchanged a look with Aisha and Zainab before nodding and embracing Asiya.

"Please sit with us, Lila," Harif said, waving her over to the couches.

Lila smiled for the first time since they arrived.

"Assad!" Zainab yelled.

Asiya's insides turned to goo at the mention of his name, and her heart started pounding so much she feared everyone else could hear her.

"Yes, yes," Harif said. "Let's surprise him. He's due to drop by after work today." He grinned at Asiya, and she busied herself with taking off her hijab, hiding her smile.

Lila fumbled with hers, wrestling with the idea of whether to take it off or not. After a few moments, she took it off, and Asiya beamed. Lila was leaning into being a member of the family.

"Wait," Harif said, throwing everyone an apologetic smile. "A moment." He picked up his phone and walked into the kitchen, dialing Jude's number.

Hearing his friend pick up, Harif said a bit too hurriedly, "She's home."

"I know. The BNI just aired the breaking news."

"I want you to know...Ameera and I are grateful for your help."

"But I didn't find her."

"You protected Assad and did all you could for us. We'd love to have lunch with you tomorrow, In Shaa Allah. If you're up for it, of course."

"I'm game. I could never say no to you."

Harif laughed, the corners of his eyes crinkling. "See you." He hung up and hurried back to the living room, his whole being feeling lighter with each step. "Thank you for waiting. Let's watch the news before you tell us what happened. I have already heard some details, but I don't mind listening again." He flipped channels until he tuned in to one of the major TV stations just in time to see the criminals.

T-Bone looked like a deer in headlights with a gash on the back of his head. The left side of his face and his shirt were soaked rouge. One by one, the camera focused on every one of Debayo's workers. The head of the BNI announced that anyone who worked for Debayo under duress would return to their families after writing statements, and the rest would be prosecuted. The families of the abducted girls would also be located, after which the girls would be returned to their homes.

Harif felt his eyes burn, and he clenched his hands into fists as each person was made to look into the camera. Ameera felt an overwhelming need to thrash the TV. Lila and Asiya only recoiled into each other, their eyes glued to the screen. With the report over, Harif switched off the TV in a huff, turning his attention to his family.

"Let's hear your story now. Wait...it seems like Assad is here." Harif stepped out as the women covered their hair with their hijabs.

Assad was allowed into the room, and his eyes found Asiya and stayed on her. Harif came up behind him, nudging him.

"She's real. But don't ignore the rest of us now that she's here," he added with a smile in his voice.

Everyone laughed, but the couple didn't take their eyes off each other even as Assad was made to sit by Ameera. They drew and drank each other in, wishing they could do more than just look. They saw, though. In Assad's eyes, Asiya saw his fears melt, and their warmth increased in intensity until she could feel their heat. Asiya's eyes were soothing and inviting, her pupils dilating and making room for Assad. Lila stole glances at them, a dull ache in her chest.

After they'd narrated their experiences while living with Debayo—with Lila being more open to talking about her own family—Assad took his leave, and the rest of the family got ready for bed. Asiya saw him out, and they lingered at the gate, saying little in hushed voices.

"I missed you," Assad said, his sincere eyes boring into

hers. He felt the most hurting parts of him start to heal. He wouldn't take his eyes off her.

"What if I told you I missed you the most?" She yearned to hold him, her tucked-away parts coming alive.

Assad chortled. "Nobody would believe that."

"Well, I did. Deal with it."

"Did he hurt you?"

"Dad asked. I said no."

"Yes, but you could have excluded facts to make them feel better."

"He didn't, I promise. We saw each other only a few times."

Assad exhaled. "Naaji. *I've heard you.* It's good to have you back. I feel like I'll finally have a good night's sleep today."

"I suppose you will. Good night."

"Good night. I'll call you."

"You better."

They laughed. With a farewell wave, Asiya went back inside, and Assad started his car. Her joy turned bitter-sweet when she saw Lila sprawled on the sofa, looking like she was in a daze. It broke her heart—escaping wasn't a reason for Lila to be wholly happy again. Her family was gone. The boy she thought she would build another one with was gone, too.

"Hey..." Asiya said, walking toward Lila.

"Hi," Lila replied, looking up at Asiya with a smile. But there was something behind it, something sad.

"Want to talk about it?" Asiya asked.

"I guess." She fiddled with her fingers, biting her bottom lip hard. "So...umm...I always thought I'd be at peace and happy if I ever left Debayo's mansion. He deserves to return to whatever hell he crawled out of, but peace has eluded me. I know it hasn't yet been a while since we escaped, and I need to give it time, but right now, I feel lost. I feel as empty as I felt when I lived in that godforsaken house—if not more." She sniffled and continued talking, her voice breaking. "I miss Mami and Baba terribly, and I can't help but think of how different my life is going to be now. Your family has accepted me, and I'm grateful, but I know—I think—I will always be an 'other.' I will always feel Mami and Baba's absence. Nothing that happens to Debayo will ever be enough. Nothing will ever make my heart light again."

"Oh," Asiya said, and when Lila looked at her, she realized she was crying too.

"You're crying. I am sorry for venting like this. I should've kept all that to myself. It'll get better, I think."

"No, no," Asiya said, wiping her eyes with the back of her hand. "I am glad you've confided in me. And I'm sorry you have to go through this. Truth is, I would've cried myself to sleep tonight. What you said triggered the tears to come earlier than I wanted them to." She chuckled.

Lila held Asiya's hand. "Want to talk about it?"

"Therapy session much?" Asiya chuckled again.

"You don't have to make jokes about it to feel better, you know. Tell me how you feel, and we'll get through it together."

Asiya sniffed. "I feel like everything that's happened is my fault. I've been blaming myself since I was abducted. My mind keeps telling me *it's your fault. Your looks got you here. You endangered everyone you care about.* I try to tell myself that I didn't ask to be born this way and that Debayo should be the one to blame. He is the monster that got attracted to my looks and was willing to kill to make me his."

She stopped talking and buried her face in her hands, sobbing quietly. Lila pulled Asiya close to her. After a moment, Asiya pulled back, wiping her eyes with the end of her hijab.

"You know, the more I learned of him, the more I realized he was not bewitched to be the beast he was, but that he was a beast by choice. He deserves every punishment sent his way."

Lila held Asiya's hand and nodded her agreement. There wasn't much else to say now that they had spilled out the largest darkness from their hearts. They sat alone in the living room, each lost in her emotions.

About an hour later, Lila looked up at Asiya with glassy eyes and, in a hoarse whisper, told her she wanted to visit her old home to get her things.

CHAPTER 19

DEBAYO SAT with his hands tied behind his chair, and thick, blackish blood snaked down his nose and into his mouth. The chief of the BNI sat across the brown table from him, knuckles bloody. Debayo's resistance was waning—it wouldn't be long until he admitted his crimes and exposed his partners.

The cell was dimly lit, but one could easily tell that the white walls were dirty and needed re-painting. The chief looked down at his blue uniform, dotted with Debayo's blood. He hated having to torture criminals no more than he hated wearing his uniform for it, but seasoned criminals like Debayo would only provide information when in deep pain.

Finally, when his eyes half closed and he looked on the verge of passing out, he said it.

"Please."

"'Please' what?"

"My daughter. She's in Canada. I'll tell you everything if you protect her."

"Okay. Tell me. I'll place a few calls and get back to you."

"No. Quid pro quo. You need me as much as I need you. Make sure my daughter is safe first."

The chief looked at the deteriorating man for a while and then stood. He was right. They needed each other. Besides, this was going better than expected. For a man who'd been hunted for half of his adult life, Debayo was too ready to be loose-lipped. But even the chief would've done the same if it would keep his daughter alive.

"What province is she in? And any specifics?"

Debayo smiled, despite the heaviness that had settled in the pit of his belly. "Nova Scotia. Highway 118. Her name's Tomi."

The chief exited the cell to speak with people he knew would be able to help him find Tomi, and then returned to Debayo's cell, unable to look him in the eye. There would be no need to search for Tomi.

"Tell me." Debayo's voice was several octaves lower, gruff, and cold.

"They...got to her first. I'm sorry."

Debayo's bitter laugh rang through the little cell.

"Sorry? I'm not entirely surprised. It's what they do, the blasted murderers."

"You're a murderer yourself."

He sighed. "Get me a pen and paper. You'll need addresses."

After Debayo wrote the addresses and names of his accomplices, the chief retied his hands again and left the cell. An hour later, he returned.

"You have a visitor."

Debayo raised his head and saw him. He'd watched him from afar, but he looked more dangerous up close. Jude remained at the gate and looked at this powerful man who was now close to his grave.

When Jude didn't speak for a full couple of minutes, Debayo grew uncomfortable. "Have you come to gloat? Go ahead, have at me. There's very little I can do."

"No."

"No?"

Jude moved closer, seating himself at the edge of the table. "I didn't come to gloat. I just wanted to see the man who evaded the best investigators in the country for decades."

"You mean yourself."

"I suppose."

"There isn't much to see now, is there? I'm a dead man, Jude. That should be satisfying enough for you."

Jude was surprised and, at the same time, not very surprised Debayo knew his name. He was, after all, an intelligent criminal. "Not quite."

"You mean you didn't get to capture me."

Jude bobbed his head in a tentative nod. "The rumors are true. You *are* intelligent."

"Not intelligent enough, apparently. Two girls cornered me when I thought I was beyond the grasp of everyone, big and small."

"How does it feel?" Jude cocked his head, locking gazes with Debayo.

Debayo laughed briefly. "The defeat? We are opposite sides of the same coin, but tell me. How are you taking this failure?"

"Not very well."

"There's your answer. Men like us hate failure, even if it's well-deserved. Though, I must hand it to them. They did quite well."

Jude grunted and got up, not sparing the prisoner the least of glances. Debayo hung his head again. He never thought this day would come. The day when he would see and feel death, the day when the end would feel scarier than he had imagined.

His little girl was gone—there was nothing to live for anymore. The tears finally came when he remembered the first time he had set his eyes on her. She was a beautiful little thing and grew into a pure, elegant woman. She was good, even to bullies. He'd give the world just to see his little girl again.

I FORCE my eyes open and sit up. I close my eyes again, and I see what used to be my home. I see Mami and Baba sitting on a couch, holding each other like it's the only thing that matters. It *is* the only thing that matters. Only, they're not really here. And I'm alone, albeit having a new family. It's a feeling that will never truly leave me.

I leave the bed and make my way to the bathroom. I make wudhu and pray fajr. Asiya enters as I remain seated on the prayer mat, making du'a for Mami and Baba.

She waits until I'm done, and I've lowered my hand before she draws the curtains. She returns to the bed, and I turn to face her and look around the room. It's beautiful. It's hard to believe the family didn't decorate this room with me in mind because it gives off a minimalist vibe, which I'm all for.

Asiya tells me to get ready—she wants to go with me to my old home. I have in mind to fetch Mami's old journal, our documents, and any other thing I can't leave behind.

She leaves to get ready, leaving a pair of jeans and a shirt behind, and a yellow floral hijab. I get dressed and look at myself in the mirror before I step out. I don't see the plain woman I'm used to seeing, and it feels surreal. The woman staring back at me looks like she's making her way home to herself.

After breakfast, we set off. Asiya's dad—now my dad—had some misgivings about us going off alone, so he called an Uber for us. Not that I blame him. Debayo has been arrested, but who knows how many other deranged murderers lurk in the shadows.

When we arrive, I leave the car and take tentative steps toward my old house. I feel so alien. Asiya follows close behind, clutching my hand in hers. The street is deserted as usual, and I don't see any familiar faces. Thinking about it, I don't want to see any of these people. They stood there and watched Debayo do as he pleased. They could've called the police. Mami was good to every one of them; it was the least they could have done.

There's a stick holding the lock in place. I remove it and push the front door open. It's just as I remember; only it looks like dust was rained on it. I walk straight to the living room and stop in my tracks. Baba's body isn't there, but I can still see the blood, dried and dark red and ugly. The room smells of things that have gone bad, dust, and death.

I stifle a sob and walk to their bedroom before I lose it. I pass my hand over the white bed sheet, now turned brown and dusty. Mami had breathed her last right at this spot.

I kneel and pull out the box Baba stored important documents in. Asiya kneels close to me and looks on as I peruse the documents. I set aside the ones I want to take with me—my birth certificate and that of my parents, school documents, and health insurance—it's almost every paper in the box. And then, I see the thing I wanted to look for—Mami's journal. It's old, and half of the pages have come off the spine.

I sit on the dirty carpet, disregarding my clothes, and Asiya does the same. I love that she's quiet and looking on, holding my hand intermittently. I flip through; I'm not looking for anything in particular, but I can't help it. I run my fingers across the partially faded ink, and at this moment, Mami is alive. And I'm with her.

I come to an entry and halt. It's dated 24th February 1996, a week after I was born. I go some pages back and look for an entry on the day I was born or the days following that. I find none. I flip the pages back to the entry on 24th and begin to read.

24-02-1996

Allah has finally answered our duas. We got a call from the orphanage about a child. Her mother brought her in just yesterday. Alice says she thinks the mother can't take care of it. Says she looked weird when she gave her up. Anyway, I went with the husband for the paperwork. We returned home earlier with her (he's reading a newspaper in the living room, and my daughter is asleep). So, that's how come I have the liberty to write this. Alice said her mother named her Harissa, but I want to name her Lila.

We'll have her birth certificate and everything done soon. Alhamdulillah, a million times. I'm finally a mother! We are finally parents! I wondered on the way home if I'll tell her one day that she was adopted. But it's too early to let it bother me. I'll know what to do when the time comes, In Shaa Allah. Starting today, I'll no more feel ashamed to show up at gatherings. I have a child now! I wish I could scream it to the world. Other women will no longer make me the topic of this town's gossip. They will no longer call me barren and make hurtful remarks about the husband or myself. I won't feel less of a woman anymore.

. . .

I'm free now, Alhamdulillah. This page is wet. I can't help it, though I'm trying to be quiet not to wake her or upset the husband.

Ayman

I place the journal on my lap and wipe off the tears threatening to fall in torrents before I turn to face Asiya.

"Did you read it?" she asks.

"I started to but realized it was personal, so I stopped."

I pass the journal to her, and she looks at me again for confirmation before she reads the entry. When she's done, she looks up at me, mouth agape.

"Yep...same," I say. I don't know what I'm feeling. I *am* feeling something, but I can't name it. I'm not even mad Mami never told me. I'm happy she lived her life as my mami to the fullest—birth mother or not.

"How?"

"She didn't live long enough to tell me. That's how."

"No...not that. You're Harissa. And you're older than I am. Oh, God."

"Huh? What are you saying?"

Asiya's eyes are wide, and her voice is frantic.

"Harissa. My older sister, I think. I didn't tell you about her. But my mum gets...episodes. Each time, she mentions this name over and over again. I guessed...we guessed...Aisha, Zainab, and I, that Mother gave birth to her years before she gave birth to me. We always assumed she died or something. But it looks like Harissa may be you. And you may be her."

"Wait...what?" I don't think I've heard her right.

"It's a lot to take in, I know. I can't believe it myself."

"Wow."

"Yeah. Wow."

We sit in silence for a few minutes, thinking about Mami's words about my birth mother, before I speak again. "I don't think I want to go back to your house."

Asiya hesitates, and her face is cloudy. She looks like she's battling something. "What are you talking about? It's your house now too."

"No. This is my home. Why would she want me now if she gave me up for adoption?"

"Again, it's just my theory. I could be wrong—"

"Or you could be right."

"Yes. Or that. But Mother has suffered. You're wrong in thinking she wouldn't want you or didn't want you if I'm right."

"She still left me with strangers."

"Strangers who took care of you as your birth parents would have. Lila...please. Let's go home and get her to tell us if I'm right or not. Before you do anything else."

Without another word, I get up and make a feeble

attempt at cleaning the dirt off my bum. I pick up the papers and the journal and make my way out. I stop briefly to look at Baba's blood again before I leave my house. Asiya follows suit soon after, and she calls us an Uber. She peers at the driver's face before settling in the back seat.

When we arrive at the house, Asiya's mother, who could also be my mother, is setting the table for supper. Asiya says something to her. She looks at me strangely and joins us in the living room.

"Mother," Asiya begins the moment her mother is seated. "What happened to Harissa?"

Her mother wipes her hand on her apron. She looks nervous as hell.

"Mother—"

"I heard you." She wipes her hand some more and averts Asiya's eyes to look at her hands resting in her lap. "Why do you want to know?"

"Because she may be Harissa," Asiya says, nodding in my direction. She's so straightforward that it throws me off momentarily.

Her mother inhales sharply, and her eyes never leave mine. Not until she's done narrating the truths surrounding my birth and adoption.

CHAPTER 21

AMEERA LIVED in a small house in Kaneshie with her parents. The house had two rooms; the bedroom where her mother and father slept and the main room that held the bulky television where she slept. Six months after her eighteenth birthday, Ameera died for the first time. It was a death that began slowly, with bits and pieces of her being chiseled off until nothing was left.

It started with Nazif.

She met him a month after turning eighteen, and for the following months, she couldn't contain her heart in her chest. It fought to be out in the open, and her heart went into overdrive every time she saw him.

He was the first man to hold her heart and entire being in his palm. Ameera was fascinated by him. Anytime they had a rendezvous two blocks away from her house in the darkness, she stared at his perfection. When he caught her staring, she smiled so that pits appeared on her cheeks.

On one of such meetings, Nazif made a suggestion that caused a fine sheen of sweat to cover Ameera's forehead. She loved him, but she was scared out of her wits.

He wanted her to visit him at his house.

Ameera's mother had told her stories of girls visiting men and waking up the following day with the seed of the men within them. As uneasy as his suggestion made her, she concluded he was not of the men who do as her mother warned. Nazif was the sweet young man she'd known for five months with a future to his name—they were both done with secondary school and awaiting their acceptance letters into the university—so she agreed to his request.

She left the house early on the scheduled day to wait for Nazif by the roadside. Ameera told her mother before setting off that her friend Suzzy, who was still in secondary school, needed help with some schoolwork. All the while she told the lie, her tongue turned and threatened to reveal her deceit. She was terrible at lying, and when her mother looked at her with disapproval, she considered confessing.

The moment her mother bobbed her head in a slight nod, Ameera turned on her heels lest her lie be smelled. She passed by Suzzy's house to tell her what she was doing. Suzzy laughed and swatted Ameera's small arm, telling her to relax because she didn't really lie—she did just visit her friend, after all, didn't she?

Ameera left Suzy's house, a bundle of nerves, and waited at the next junction for her boyfriend to pick her up. No sooner had she stood there that he appeared up the road, swaggering towards her. The trepidation returned, and she wiped her hands on her skirt.

When Nazif got to her, he grinned as he towered over her. He swooped down to kiss her forehead like he always did when he saw her, and her belly flipped upside down. They held hands, and he led her through some brushes and to his house. It was a small, decent house, much like Ameera's. He had his own room, though, and she followed him into it.

Ameera was lovestruck and knew things happened when a girl was alone with a boy. She didn't know exactly what *things*, but she knew they were things the body responded to. And she knew where it would lead to—sin.

None of those things happened. Not on that day, nor on the other days she visited him after it. The more she visited him, the more Ameera wanted it to happen—she was hyperaware whenever they were close. She wanted to know what it felt like, but her cautiousness outweighed her curiosity. Her boyfriend seemed to understand.

And it only spiked her awe of him. She grew more

confident in her lover by the day and more secure in her supposition of safety.

A few days after their university acceptance letters were mailed, Ameera snuck out to her boyfriend's house to celebrate. They were accepted into different universities but were confident it wouldn't harm their relationship.

When she entered his room, it was dark, and he was sprawled in front of his small television, watching her favorite show. He grinned and motioned for her to join him. She did and rested her head on his shoulder.

In the middle of watching the show, he switched off the television and turned to her, his eyes wet. She was shocked by his abruptness and more so by his glistening eyes and single trails of tears on each cheek. She cupped his face in her hands and her brows knitted in a frown.

"What is it? Are you hurt?" Her words were barely corrigible. Her confusion had constricted her throat.

He looked deep into her eyes, the wetness sticking to his cheeks, and then pushed her down. Still looking into her eyes, he began to tear at her clothes.

Wide-eyed in shock, her eyes pleaded with him, her voice disintegrated from her throat, but he turned into someone else—something else. There was nothing human about the way he flung the shreds of her clothes. His glazed-over eyes were unreadable.

She would never understand why he did this to her.

. . .

Ameera dragged herself off the floor and limped to her house, grateful for the darkness. She had felt herself die and shrouded herself in shame as boundless as the night sky above her.

She slipped into her house through the backdoor of the kitchen, making a beeline for the bathroom. She spent the next few hours there, letting the water mix with her tears. She scrubbed her body until her skin was raw, yet still felt dirty after.

Gimbiya came out of her bedroom just as Ameera exited the bathroom.

"Anh anh. Ameera. You're back. I didn't hear you come in. You stayed over at Suzzy's too long today." The woman wiped her hands over her worn cloth dress and peered at Ameera's face as if she was inspecting it.

"Yes, Mother. There was a lot to teach." She kept her eyes on the dirty wall behind her mother.

"Ohh, I see. Toh, I hope she's learning hard. Suzzy wants to waste her life remaining in secondary school. Soon you girls will have to marry and bear us grandchildren, you know."

Ameera shifted. Her mother loved talking about marriage and children more than anything. Before she could launch into yet another lecture on how the essence of a woman is in marriage and children and not education, Ameera jumped to her friend's defense.

"Suzzy is taking school seriously this time around, mother." Ameera smiled, imagining Suzzy's hysterical laughter at this statement. She would find it funny because she *wasn't* putting in extra effort, and Ameera was visiting her boyfriend instead of teaching her. "You'll see."

Suzzy didn't give a fig about school. She was certain her beauty and her parents' money would get her where she wanted.

And she was beautiful. She was dark and plump and had almond-shaped eyes. She would wiggle and roll her hips when she saw men she was interested in. When the men stared long enough, she would pass comments that made them wish they could grab her there and then.

Suzzy lived with her eighty-year-old blind grand-mother while her parents lived and worked in Switzerland. She did as she pleased, since her grandmother stayed in her room all day. Their house was twice the size of Ameera's, and she brought men home often.

She was Ameera's only friend.

Gimbiya and her husband had objected to the friend-ship in its early stages, but after they realized that their daughter would remain "good," they gave up trying to keep their daughter from Suzzy.

"I hope you're right. I don't like telling you how proud

I am because I don't want people to think I have spoiled you rotten. But you know, I'm proud you're not like Suzzy even though you two are close. You make me proud every day, my daughter. The day you bring a man home, I'll wear white from the top of my head to my toes!" She laughed, patting the air between her and her daughter.

I'm proud you're not like Suzzy.

Each word sent a dagger through her heart.

You make me proud every day, my daughter.

Each dagger turned on its axis, killing more and more of her, over and over again.

Ameera opened her mouth, wishing she could tell her mother she was no more the good daughter. That she was not even good for education now, with the long road she always envisioned when she thought about her future was breaking bit by bit, the fear of getting pregnant suffocating her. No 'good' man would want her. She was a disgrace—the same as Suzzy.

The guilt was taking up space in her mind and dragging fear along with it. If she didn't bleed the next month, she'd be as good as dead. Her father would say otherwise, but he cared about his reputation more than her happiness and well-being. Every time he talked about her education, there were shadows of a warning lurking behind his words because he, too, wanted Ameera to marry and be a good wife to her husband like her mother was to her father.

The first time he had spoken out his thoughts, his wife assured him that their daughter was responsible. She would be educated so that his prestige would overshadow his friends'. Since then, he left his threats hanging. But she felt it—it pierced into her body and made a home in her in the form of fear. If she dared disgrace him, she would cease to be his daughter.

She blinked back tears as her mother went on and on about how she wanted beautiful grandchildren. Especially so that her friends would respect her. Gimbiya had lost half their respect and her womanhood when, two years after Ameera was born, she failed to conceive again. She had two miscarriages and one stillborn child. People mocked her behind her back, and those who did still follow her only did so in the expectation that she would again give their mouths something to talk about.

Her husband's family tried coercing him to marry a second wife and ensure more children, specifically boys. When he refused, they resorted to asking him indirectly to kick his wife out or get other women pregnant out of wedlock. When he stood his ground because he respected Gimbiya for everything else, they turned on his wife. They never let go of an opportunity to make her feel small.

The family's faith made it all the more impossible for Ameera to see a way out. The daughter of a godly couple stripped of her dignity? People would crane their necks into the house just to catch a whiff of the family's sudden indignity. All the other mothers and community aunties were sure to use her as an example if her plight became public. And they were definitely going to use the age-old advice, "God doesn't listen to the prayers of girls who allow men to know their bodies."

She could almost see their mouths point to her, their faces full of condemnation and pity as they shook their heads at her and her family.

How does a girl who covers up so much give herself to a man?

What kind of mother doesn't teach her daughter to close her legs?

She's not innocent, after all. She's not married yet, but she knows the pleasures of the body.

Ameera could hear them in her mind, talking and talking, until Gimbiya turned away from her. She knew because it happened to Binta, one of the neighboring girls in the town.

"Anyway, I made your favorite today, yam and garden egg stew. Your serving is on the table inside. Eat and get some rest. Your father will be home soon, and you can help me set the table for him." Her mother ended Ameera's inner monologue, and she snapped out of her trance. The older woman walked into the bathroom and left her daughter rooted in the spot and her guilt.

Ameera lifted one heavy foot in front of the other and made her way into her parents' bedroom to change into new clothes. She stood for a while, looking into the full-length mirror. She couldn't recognize the girl staring back at her. All she saw was an empty vessel.

She tore her eyes away from her reflection and put on her clothes. It still hurt. She could feel the change in the way she walked and prayed her mother wouldn't notice. She sat at their table with chipped ends and dipped her hands into the food.

After eating, she rushed to the bathroom to perform the bath ghusl, make ablution and make up her missed prayers. She stayed longest on her prayer mat that night after isha, praying that her body would reject Nazif's seed. She froze, and her heart leaped into her mouth when she heard her father's footsteps.

CHAPTER 22

HER FATHER'S voice boomed through the tiny house as he responded to her mother's greeting. Ameera stood, legs shaking, to take her father's bag. He carried a black backpack with him each day to work at the juice factory, where he repaired machines and equipment.

The two women set the table, and he sat down to eat. He washed his blackened and stubby hands before diving into his wife's food. They sat watching him as he always wanted them to.

Halfway through his meal, he stared intently at his daughter. The more she silently expressed discomfiture, the more he stared. She felt like he was cracking her open, blink by blink. Her humiliation was wrapped around her neck and squeezing every few minutes, spurred on by her father's stares.

Her mother noticed her husband staring.

"I was just telling Ameera how proud we are of her." Her mother's voice was light and excited.

Her father grunted and nodded, returning his attention to his meal. Ameera could hear the words he didn't speak out loud.

Don't you dare disgrace me.

Her mother retreated into the bedroom, and her father followed suit after taking a shower. Ameera cleared the table and did the dishes, her mind on Suzzy.

She was suddenly envious of how Suzzy didn't care about the things that were said about her. She knew men's bodies, and she never tried to hide it.

Ameera's hand reached up to touch the cheek Nazif had slapped. Her eyes welled up, and she snatched her hand away as her cheek burned it, leaving a foam of soap on her cheek. She decided to confide in Suzzy about her little death.

She finished her chores and lay on the old couch, which served as her bed, and felt like it would crumble at any moment. She lay awake longer than she intended—her eyes would just not shut—thin streaks of tears snaked down the sides of her eyes into her ears.

His face hovered above in the darkness of the living room, sneering down at her curled body. She turned facedown, burying herself in the soft and dank couch. She pressed her face hard into it so that the cushion muffled her sniffles. Soon, her tears dried up, and sleep claimed her. So did the nightmares about Nazif—and of another's face she'd tried to forget but resurfaced now that it had happened again.

The sound of her mother dragging her feet woke her up. Ameera prayed fajr and hurried through her chores. When her father walked out the front door, she bid her mother goodbye and left through the backdoor.

She arrived at Suzzy's house, palms clammy and head swimming. She pushed the heavy front door open and stepped onto the furry carpet. Suzzy's grandmother sat perched on one sofa, clutching her walking stick.

She craned her neck as if trying to see who had just entered the room. Before she could open her mouth, Ameera cleared her throat.

"It's me, Naana. Ameera."

Naana nodded, the features on her wrinkled face softening in recognition. "I haven't...err...seen you around lately. How is your mother?" Her voice was cracked and strained.

"She's well, Naana. How are you feeling? Suzzy told me you had taken ill."

"Yes, yes. You know old age comes along with its own...err...afflictions. It'll end soon. I don't know why I'm still alive." She laughed briefly and then hung her head as a coughing bout took over. She raised her head back up, swiping a bony hand over her lips. "Hurry along now, child. My granddaughter is still in her room." Her chest caved in and puffed out with each breath and word.

Ameera shuffled past her and repeatedly looked over her shoulder, even when the old woman was well out of her view. There was a rush of sympathy and dismay each time she saw or spoke to the old woman. It didn't help that Suzzy grumbled each time her grandmother needed her.

Ameera reached Suzzy's brown door. She sighed and pushed it open. Suzzy stopped tapping her feet in tune with an American song and raised an eyebrow when Ameera walked in and slumped beside her on the bed.

"What's up, A-girl?" she asked as Ameera removed her hijab and began turning it in her hand. "You look like you've been hit by a truck."

"Suzzy, my cherry has been popped." The words were swift, and Ameera's eyes never left her hands as she said them, but Suzzy saw her shiver.

"Girl! Was it Mr. Loverman? How was it? I bet it was painful. But don't worry, it gets better and better with time. And 'my cherry has been popped'? How old are you, seventy?" She nudged Ameera and winked, a huge smile on her face. Despite the smile on her face, she felt something was not right.

When Ameera remained silent and lifted a finger to

dub the tears at the corners of her eyes, Suzzy's big eyes widened now that her worries were realized.

"He didn't hurt you, did he? Please, say something. Tell me he didn't do anything to you." Suzzy was panicking now. She sat up to face Ameera, trying and failing to hide her shaking hands.

"He raped me." Ameera's voice was so quiet, Suzzy wasn't sure she heard her right. The tears bathing Ameera's cheeks confirmed that she hadn't lost her hearing.

"That moron! How dare he? Wait until I get my hands on his filthy self. I'll squeeze every bit of life out of his useless body." Suzzy balled her hands into fists and swallowed hard. Her face felt hot, and her eyes stung. Why did this have to happen to the one person she truly cared for?

"Suzzy, do you remember Uncle Hassan?"

"Yes, love. I do. How on earth could I forget?" Suzzy couldn't stop the tears from escaping.

"He— he—"

"Shhh, love, I know," Suzzy cooed. She wrapped her arms around Ameera and rubbed her back in soothing circles. The tears weren't flowing as much as before, and Suzzy felt like she was going to burst.

Long before Nazif had his way with Ameera, Hassan had chipped off parts of her over and over. Hassan was her father's friend and had lobbied for her father to secure a job at the factory.

He visited the family frequently and would stay the whole evening. He would eat with the family and trade banter with Ameera's father. He hardly paid Ameera any attention before she turned sixteen. He only asked her about school and patted her head after talking with her.

That all changed on Ameera's sixteenth birthday. He visited as usual and wished her a year filled with goodness when her parents informed him of the event. He did more than wish her goodness, however.

His eyes first searched her face, then traveled across her maturing body, stopping at the places that were gathering fullness. His eyes never left her body, even when she sat in the corner and pretended she didn't exist. Even when his mouth spoke with her parents, his eyes bore into her. It continued for a week, and Ameera had only Suzzy to express her growing uneasiness.

A week later, he visited at an unusual time—when he knew Ameera's father was still at work and her mother was shopping at the market. Ameera let him into the house, and he made himself comfortable on a couch. She served him some water from the small fridge in the kitchen and watched him keenly as he gulped it down. His bald head and dark face were wet with sweat. He placed the handkerchief he was holding and beckoned Ameera to sit beside him.

His lips stretched into a yellow-toothed smile when she hesitated, saying he only wanted to ask her a few questions. Ameera sat beside him as he asked, and before long, his hands were in her underwear. He pushed her so that she lay on the couch and held her in place with one large arm, his palm clasping her lips shut.

It hurt, and she was sobbing by the time he pulled his hands away. He showed her a knife tucked away among his shirts in his backpack and warned her to shut up about what he did.

Soon after, Ameera's mother returned, and Hassan made a good show of pretending he had been waiting for her and her husband. Ameera shook like a leaf the entire time, waiting to come undone and cry into the couch.

Hassan defiled her for months—and whenever he did, she sought comfort in Suzzy —until he left the country for Nigeria.

Ameera had once considered confiding in her parents, but she knew what their responses would be. Her mother would say it was impossible, circling an arm over her head and snapping her fingers as she did. Her father would simply tell her not to be an ingrate and liar—they owed their livelihood to the man. He would tell her to cover herself more and admonish her mother for not training her to be respectful and decent.

"Woman!" he would yell. Her mother would startle the way she did whenever he yelled, running to his side to listen to what he had to say and do his bidding.

"Teach your daughter to be a good woman. I shouldn't have to do your duty for you. Am I clear?" He would stroke his beard and wait for her to talk back. She wouldn't, of course, lest he strike her.

They'd sweep it under the rug, and her wounds would fester beyond salvaging.

CHAPTER 23

AMEERA DIDN'T SEE any blood the following month. Her mother picked up on it because she usually suffered severe period cramps. On the last day of the month, Gimbiya called her daughter into the bedroom after her husband left for work.

The summon filled Ameera with dread—her guts screamed that her mother knew something, but her mind told her it could be anything at all. She entered her parents' bedroom, eyes on the carpeted floor.

"Sit," her mother said, patting the space beside her on the bed.

Ameera did as she was bid, and her mother looked at her as if deciding what to say.

"Won't you go to the market today, Mother?" her voice betrayed her and laid bare all that she felt inside.

"Have you bled this month?"

Ameera gulped, all her thoughts and words sinking into her belly. She shook her head, holding her trembling hands in her lap.

"And is there something I need to know? Something you should've told me?"

Ameera summoned all the strength she had to push the words out of her belly. "I got raped, mother." The words left a metallic taste in her mouth.

"By whom? And how and when did it happen?" Gimbiya was outraged and afraid; her voice was loud, but her hands were shaking.

"I—" she wet her lips and looked past her mother at the photo of her parents hanging above the bed. "I was seeing him, and one day when I visited him—"

Her mother raised her eyebrows. Ameera could taste the disappointment on her mother's face.

"He held me on the floor and raped me." Her eyes were wet, and snot glided down her nostril. She tore her eyes from the photo to find her mother crying with her hands on her head and her bosom heaving. "I'm sorry, mother. I loved him, and I thought we'd get married. I'm sorry."

"Your father has to know." She couldn't meet her daughter's eyes.

"No. Please, Mother," Ameera gasped and wheezed,

the tears flowing in torrents. "Don't tell him. He'll kill me. Disown me."

Her mother shook her head. "He has to know. I'd forgive you and care for you and the baby, but he'd kill me if I did. We're both at his mercy."

That evening, she sat with her mother and waited for her father to finish eating. When he did, he reclined on the couch and belched. He rubbed his fat belly and looked at his wife and daughter. The contentment on his face was unmistakable.

Ameera chewed her lips and fidgeted, throwing her mother pleading looks every now and then. Her mother's lips were downturned, and she clasped and unclasped her hands, gauging her husband's mood.

"My beautiful family," he drawled. "Why do you two look like there's something you need to tell me? Speak up, speak up. Don't be afraid. What's a man who terrifies his family? A monster!" His raucous laughter rang through the house. "And I'm no monster. So, what do you want to tell me? Let's hear it."

Gimbiya unclasped her hands and placed each on her knees. She took a deep breath and looked at Ameera before forcing her lips apart.

"Dear husband," she began.

Her husband laughed again, slapping his palm against the arm of the couch. He turned to Ameera. "You know, all these years with your mother, and I can still read her. She always calls me 'dear husband' when she needs something badly. Women!" He laughed again.

Ameera tried to smile, but the muscles in her face wouldn't relax. He was right. He could see through her mother, but you could never tell with him. His fury was a fire that swallowed everything in its path that could be lit by the simplest things.

"Go on, woman. I need to rest for tomorrow. Some big machines need repairing."

"Ameera— our daughter...she hasn't bled this month."

"And is that a cause for concern? Do you need money for the hospital? This is a woman's matter, you know."

"No. It's...it's not that. She might be pregnant."

Ameera recoiled into herself—she would enter the couch if she could. Her father's face had clouded over, threatening to pour out all the rage. He stood up slowly, inching towards his daughter.

He crouched beside her, their faces only inches apart. "Tell me that what your mother said is a lie." His voice dripped with disgust.

Ameera opened her mouth and closed it. She could only cry her eyes out.

"Habba," Gimbiya said, exasperated. "For God's sake, she was raped. Please, try and understand. It wasn't her fault. Please." She left the couch and stepped closer to her husband, attempting to place a hand on his shoulder. He stood up abruptly and sent his wife's hand flying. His hand came down on her cheek when she didn't move away. She stumbled a few steps back, placing a shaking hand over the stinging area.

"You raised her to be a whore. Raped or not, she's a disgrace. My daughter can never be a disgrace. This one is no more my kin. Get her out of my sight!" Heaving with the strength of his words, he looked like he could crush both mother and daughter into fine specks of nothingness.

"Where would she go now? She's our only daughter. Please, forgive her; I'll take care of the baby."

"Shut your conniving mouth before I send you away, too!" The intensity of his words and body warmed the room, despite the smell of the wet earth outside. "I will not be taken for a fool. Do you hear me?" He stormed out of the living room into the bedroom and slammed the door so hard it rattled in its frame.

Mother and daughter sat, each lost in their thoughts, and dozed off on the couches until the wee hours of the morning. They were startled awake by the slamming of the bedroom door. Ansar stood in front of the door, his hands in his pockets.

"I told you to get her out of my sight. What is she still doing here?" He wouldn't look at his daughter. "If I find her in this house when I'm back from the factory, you leave with her. Am I clear?" Without waiting for a response or reaction, he walked past them and into the bathroom. He left the house half an hour later without looking at his family or asking for a hearty breakfast to start his day.

Gimbiya dragged herself to the bathroom and returned to her seat in the living room. Ameera did the same, shooting her mother petrified looks.

"Go and pack. I'll escort you," she said, unable to meet her daughter's eyes.

"To where? Mother, I'd rather he killed me with his bare hands than leave. Where will I go?"

"Suzzy's."

Ameera let out a dry laugh, her face contorting in pain. "You don't even like her. I'm sure you think I've turned out like her because she's my only friend."

"Be careful, girl. I'm your only parent now. Don't talk to me like you would your friend," Gimbiya said, looking at her daughter sharply.

"I'm sorry." She returned from her parents' bedroom with a bag filled with clothes and toiletries to meet her mother clutching at her cloth, all the while sobbing quietly.

When Gimbiya sensed her daughter's presence, she dabbed her eyes dry and tightened the cloth around her waist. She stepped out of the house with her daughter, bolted the door, and dropped the rusty key into the small purse wedged under her armpit.

Before she slept last night, Gimbiya had a mind to confront her daughter's rapist. But the chances of him running off and spreading the news while it was still at the root level were so high that she talked herself out of it.

She led the way, and her daughter followed, each praying not to be spotted. A few people did, however; as expected, their eyes followed them and their lips moved.

Gimbiya waited outside while Ameera went inside with her bag when they arrived. After what seemed like an eternity, Ameera and Suzzy came out. Gimbiya's patience had worn thin by then. She glared at them and said nothing.

"Good day, ma. Welcome. Shall I get you some water?" Suzzy said, looking from the older woman to her perfect nails and back again. Ameera shifted at her friend's obvious false courtesy.

Gimbiya simply sighed and shook her head. "In my heart of hearts, I don't want my daughter to stay here. I know I'll bite my fingers later, but you're her only hope now. She's not safe with her father. I've seen how violent he can get—"

"And yet, you married him anyway," Suzzy said. She stood akimbo, a frown directed at Gimbiya.

"Suzzy!" Ameera nudged her friend, and her hand flew over her mouth.

"I don't blame you, but I'm not here to condemn you.

Take care of my daughter. I'll drop by when I can and get you whatever you need." With that, Gimbiya walked off, swallowing the thickness that was lodged in her throat and causing her to gasp.

The road stretched before her like it was never-ending, and her tears blurred her vision. She walked on the road and was narrowly missed by a truck carrying plantains. The driver hurled insults at her and drove off. She moved to the sidewalk and continued her journey home.

Suzzy left Ameera with her grandmother and went out under the pretext of meeting one of her lovers for an urgent matter. Suzzy walked towards Nazif's excuse of a house, her pace quickening as she approached the brushes right in front of it.

She knocked until her knuckles were sore, but the door was locked. She removed the scrunchie around her wrist and used it to tie her waist-length box braid, deciding to go back home and return later. When she turned to leave, she caught a whiff of cigarette and walked in the direction of the smell. She was met with Nazif's friend leaning on a tree with a joint between his thin lips.

"Where's your friend?"

"Bush girl. Didn't anyone teach you how to greet?"

Suzzy bristled, and she walked closer to him, fists raised and nostrils flaring. "Where's your idiot friend? You either tell me, or I make sure you're unable to smoke for weeks or months."

"Relax. I've heard about how you beat all the guys who tried to touch you before you started sleeping around." He laughed, blowing smoke into her face. No sooner had the laughter died out than his left cheek stung. Suzzy hit him again, and he staggered sideways away from the withered tree.

"Do I need to ask again?"

"I don't know. He said something about quitting school and starting a business. He left this morning. And I don't know where."

Suzzy sized him up for a moment. He looked too shaken to be lying. She weighed her options. As much as she wanted to put Nazif through pain for hurting her friend, she needed to keep the pregnancy a secret. "The moment he returns, alert me. Have you heard?" Without waiting for a response, she raised her hand. "I'm sure I can count on you. You have a good enough reminder."

She returned to her house and reported her findings to Ameera. Ameera listened, growing more worried by the minute. She asked Suzzy to let it go—her father was enough for her to deal with.

"No." Suzzy shook her head. "I haven't ever said no to you, but now, I have to. I won't rest until the animal gets what he deserves. He better remain wherever he is, or he's as good as dead."

Ameera stayed in the room next to Suzzy's. She was elated about having her own room, albeit under unfortunate circumstances. Suzzy informed her grandmother of her friend's stay, claiming it was to help her with schoolwork. The old woman's eyes flickered in disbelief, but she only nodded and returned to listening to her old radio.

Ameera stayed in her room all day, every day. She prayed at their stipulated times and sat on a chair or her bed instead of standing to pray when the pregnancy grew heavy. In the mornings, Suzzy drew a bath and helped her with anything she needed, often checking in on her at random times of the day. If Suzzy's grandmother knew about the pregnancy, she kept it to herself.

Ameera stayed with Suzzy until the day she pushed out her baby. People were already coining stories and persecuting Suzzy more than before. It didn't bother Suzzy, and she spent a great amount of time trying to convince Ameera to be less bothered by them.

Some said Suzzy introduced her friend to the life she was living but failed to educate her on birth control. Others said Suzzy conspired with one of her many lovers to do this to her. They jeered and laughed whenever they laid eyes on Suzzy. Men rubbed their crotches and asked

Suzzy if she wanted to be with them on the condition that she brought her friend along.

Suzzy stopped men from visiting all too regularly and kept her sexual activities to a bare minimum. Instead, she spent almost all her time caring for her friend.

Gimbiya visited twice every week, first in secret and later with the knowledge of her husband. He didn't approve, but for the first time since he married his wife, he couldn't get her to do what he wanted. She sent them food and stayed for hours on end, talking to her daughter about pregnancy, childbirth, and motherhood. She never mentioned Nazif, and her daughter was most grateful for her.

If any good could come of this, it was that Suzzy's mutual anger towards Gimbiya diminished over time, and the two became the most amicable Ameera had ever seen them.

CHAPTER 24

ON THE DAY her labor contractions began, Ameera was alone at home. She knelt on the tiled floor in front of the bed and grit her teeth, sweat plastering tresses of hair to her forehead. Before long, she felt fluid snake down her inner thighs.

Ameera called Suzzy from the cell phone she got her, but her friend couldn't be reached, so she jammed a small white towel into her mouth and let out a hair-raising scream.

Suzzy returned sometime later to find her friend straddling the thin line between consciousness and unconsciousness. Panicking just the slightest, she sprinkled some cold water on Ameera's face. Right on cue, Gimbiya arrived at the scene. She gasped and instructed Suzzy to prepare for Ameera's delivery like she had taught her.

Suzzy stumbled out of the house to hail a taxi, grateful for the curtain of nightfall.

Gimbiya and Suzzy hauled Ameera into the taxi—Suzzy sat in front with the driver while Gimbiya held her daughter's head on her lap and cleaned her sweaty face in the back seat.

Ameera was wheeled into a delivery room the moment they arrived at the hospital. Her mother and friend paced the hallways of the hospital and jumped at the slightest provocation. They took turns sleeping on a bench as the hours whizzed by.

Twelve hours later, a light-skinned woman with a dirty-looking bob wig and a green belt dividing her overflowing belly into two halves motioned to Suzzy and Gimbiya to follow her. She led them into the room where Ameera was recuperating. The baby was brought to them and they each held her, one after the other.

They returned home at cockcrow— Gimbiya offered to stay with them but after she told her husband the news. She rushed back home to inform him of the birth of his granddaughter. He grunted and turned to face the wall, a hand under his cheek. Gimbiya stared at him, unsurprised, before packing some clothes into a bag and setting off again.

When she returned to the house, Suzzy was crouched by the sofa in the living room. She held her grandmother's crinkled hands in hers, sobbing quietly. Suzzy had tried to wake her up and help her to her room, but the woman neither moved nor breathed. Her grandmother was dead—she had died in her sleep while they were at the hospital.

Ameera remained in her room with her baby and her mother while mourning visitors poured in and out of the house the following week. Suzzy was torn. She hadn't liked helping her grandmother, but she loved her all the same.

A month after Ameera had her baby, Suzzy realized she hadn't checked up on her recently and thought to sit down and ask her friend how she was doing emotionally rather than the usual questions about post-partum aches or pains.

Ameera had just finished breastfeeding her daughter when Suzzy knocked and entered her room. Gimbiya had gone to the market earlier.

"Hey, A-girl. I'm sorry I haven't been there for you."

"Nonsense. You've always been there for me. I was supposed to be there for you when Naana passed, but the baby..." She shot her sleeping daughter a look. The baby was pink and so tiny that Ameera often watched her limbs in wonder. She then looked up at Suzzy. There were creases in her forehead, and her eyes looked heavy and reddened. Her playfulness was replaced by dullness and sorrow.

"I know, love." She sat on the bed next to her friend. "Have you decided on what to name her?"

"Yes. Harissa. I already told mother. She thinks it's a beautiful name. What do you think?"

"I think it's a great name. What was your inspiration?"

Ameera laughed. "I don't know. It just came to me, I guess." She looked at her friend. She had changed so much.

"Ah, I see." They remained silent for a few moments, and Suzzy asked the question Ameera dreaded answering. "How are you, A-girl? Tell me how you feel and what you think. You can tell me anything. You know that, right?"

"Well, I could say that I'm all right, but you'd see through my lie anyway. So...er, I'm not so good."

"And why do you say that?"

Ameera hesitated. "It's a lot, Suzzy."

"I have all the time in the world, love."

"Okay. Err...for starters, I snapped at Mother yesterday and today. She didn't complain. She just said she knew how I was feeling and that it was normal and would pass soon. And I feel guilty too. It weighs on me day and night, and I fear Mother can see it in my eyes." She looked down at her intertwined fingers.

"Why?"

"Why what?"

They laughed together.

"Why do you feel guilty, silly?"

"I feel like I'm going to subject Harissa to a stereotypical life. A single mother who lost her prospects of going to the university. And I fear the day when she asks me about her father."

"You can always go back to school unless you don't want to. Because you're good. You're not like me. You actually sit your butt down in a chair to study. You can be whoever you want to be. Harissa would be proud to call you her mother, I promise. And when she asks about that idiot, tell her the truth. She'll be more careful with men if you do."

Ameera chuckled. "You always know what to say. You should be a therapist or something."

"Nah, not for me. I'll probably get married and—"

"Wait. Did you just say married? Or did I hear wrong? Suzzy is talking about marriage! What has this world come to?" Ameera widened her eyes, tilting her head to the side.

"Oh, come on. Drama queen." Suzzy rolled her eyes and shrugged. "Times change and people change. Besides...I think I've found the one." She watched her friend for a reaction.

"No way! You're actually serious! Who would've thought? And who is this guy that has thawed your icy heart?"

"I hope your daughter doesn't get your drama queen trait." Their laughter erupted through the house. It was the first time they laughed together since Naana's passing. After, Suzzy sobered with a soft smile. "We met a year ago. Slept together and went on dates. You know, just the usual. It was meant to be something short-term, but the heart wants what it wants. And it's mutual."

"Whoa!" Ameera cooed, dragging the last syllable just a little bit more. "Girl, I'm so happy for you. Get married soon, will you? Harissa needs a best friend." As they laughed again, their hands found and held each other. The numbness Ameera had been feeling for the past few days grew lighter as she watched and listened to her friend.

"Thank you. We've been thinking about it, so expect an announcement soon." Suzzy's eyes lit up while she spoke, and Ameera knew she was truly in love. "But don't steer the topic away. We were talking about you." Suzzy cleared her throat and looked at her friend with her eyebrows raised.

"Oh. That." Ameera's voice resumed its earlier flatness. "I think it's postpartum depression. I have read about it before, so I'm quite familiar with the symptoms. And I'm scared."

"Shhh. Don't be. I'm here for you, okay? Always. But, tell me about the symptoms." Suzzy grew serious and concerned again.

"I cry a lot now. More than usual. And I feel hopeless. I feel like I'm a burden and everyone would be better off without me. I feel I should take my life and spare everyone the trouble..." Her voice was strained now, and her breath was ragged and shallow.

"You're not—" Suzzy made to interrupt her.

Ameera held up her hand, and Suzzy fell quiet. "Please, let me finish. Once I start, I cannot stop. And I want to tell you everything so that perhaps, I'll feel lighter."

Suzzy nodded.

"I'm always tired, and I can barely eat anything. Mother complains about it all the damn time, but I just can't bring myself to eat. And my thoughts. They scare me. I feel I'm unfit to be a mother. I take care of her, but I don't feel any connection to Harissa. I feel I don't want her. I wish I had lost her in the delivery room. I wish I had miscarried her." Ameera collapsed into herself, and her cries woke her daughter up.

Suzzy pulled her into a warm embrace. "There, there. We're going to make you better. I promise." She let go of her and got up to coo Harissa to sleep before leaving to get them lunch.

With her gone, loneliness shrouded Ameera. She lay on the bed, then paced the room, then sat on the floor. She just couldn't be still. Her thoughts wouldn't let her.

I am tired. And divided. One of me wants this baby— wants to love her and watch her grow. The other wants to either strangle or abandon her. And they are at odds. The guilt. I feel guilty whenever the murderous me surfaces. I feel so bad, like a horrible, horrible human being. But maybe, I am a horrible, horrible human being. I love her, and then I hate her. I look at her and I see him. His face, his grin, his eyes. I feel dirty and tainted, and it kills me all over again, leaving fresh wounds where no one can see them. But then, she smiles at me, clutches my index finger in her hand, and everything falls into a void. Everything but both of us. At that moment, her presence is a salve, and my heart swells with emotion. I hold her to my bosom like she's the only thing that matters. Then, it happens again. Until I feel an overwhelming urge to scream my guts out. I don't see an end if there'll ever be one. I love her. I hate her. I disgust myself. I am losing my mind. It hurts. It's draining, this endless cycle.

Somebody help.

Two mornings later, Harissa's gut-wrenching cry drew Suzzy to her friend's door and she stumbled on Ameera as she was about to press a pillow into her baby's face. Suzzy shrieked and yanked the pillow away, throwing Ameera off balance. She grabbed the baby and strode to her room next door, leaving Ameera propped up against her bed, her face wet and snotty.

They didn't speak for some days—Suzzy made her displeasure known—and Ameera was too embarrassed to look Suzzy in the eye, much less talk to her. Suzzy never left Harissa alone with her mother, and a week later, she informed Gimbiya of Ameera's attempted murder. Gimbiya was speechless. She had heard of stories of such women, but she had never envisioned it happening to her daughter.

It took another week after Suzzy confided in her for Gimbiya to sit her and Ameera down to talk about it. Before Gimbiya said anything, Ameera blurted out that she wanted to give Harissa up for adoption. Suzzy jumped at the idea and tried to talk her out of it, saying that she was already looking for a therapist for Ameera. But Ameera was adamant. It was clear she had already made up her mind and so, it was decided; Harissa was to be given up for adoption.

The next day, Suzzy went with Ameera to the orphanage in New Town. Neither spoke to each other on the way, and any passerby wouldn't be able to guess that the two women—one sitting upright with her hair and nails done and the other in carelessly-dressed fabrics and weighted by gloom—were best of friends.

The orphanage was in a secluded part of town and high-walled. It was made up of various buildings, some of which looked like classrooms. Ameera hoped no one would see them. A woman greeted them with a yellow face and black limbs, and too much red lipstick. At first, she looked from Suzzy to Ameera with disinterest but perked up when Ameera identified herself as the mother.

"She's called Harissa. Please, tell the family who'll adopt her to keep her first name." Ameera filled out a form and signed it as she made the request, then handed her daughter's birth certificate to the woman. The woman took it and the baby, a bit too hastily, and waited for her mother and wild-looking friend to leave.

Despite feeling like she was not adept at being a mother, something inside Ameera tore at her and caused her skin to burn, and she remained rooted in her spot. She wondered if she was making a mistake—one she'd spend the rest of her life wishing she could undo.

Suzzy tugged at her hijab just as Harissa began to fidget. Finally, Ameera sighed and turned in the direction of the huge black gates.

"Now, what?" Suzzy asked the moment they entered the house.

"I don't know. I—I don't feel so good. I feel like my body is on fire."

As much as Suzzy wanted to reprimand her, she felt sorry for her friend. "A good family will adopt her, I'm certain." But even she didn't believe her own words. They came out feeble and weightless. "Maybe, I should leave you alone for a while."

"Yes...yes. Thank you. I want to be...be by myself." Ameera exhaled with force. Why was she stammering?

Suzzy shut the door behind her, and Ameera suddenly felt the world crumble around her. The ruins surrounded her, and she longed to be part of it. Her eyes darted wildly around the room, and each time they fell on something that belonged to her daughter, she felt herself erupt in invisible flames.

Ansar wouldn't let his daughter return to his house— she was still a disgrace even without his granddaughter. But, after days of Gimbiya trying to convince him, he agreed to continue funding her education.

Ameera started university while living with Suzzy and her husband. In her final year, she met Harif. He was the doctor who attended to Suzzy when she fell pregnant. At first, Ameera was cautious and avoided him. But one day, she was called to her old home only to meet Harif in conversation with her parents.

Despite the years that had passed, her father still wouldn't look her in the eyes nor did he hide his disgust. Harif heard the rumors, of course, and she didn't deny it. But it didn't matter to him.

A month later, they were married.

Harif was nothing like Nazif; Ameera felt safe and peaceful with him, and he listened and cradled her for her every time of need. He knew her and the shape of her pain.

He held her with love—the very thing she'd grown fearful of—despite all the shrapnel of hurt lodged in her body. When she was him, the urge to give in to the darkness was almost nonexistent.

In no time, Ameera's heart was swelling and bursting for him. When he came to know of her feelings, Harif wanted to take care of Harissa. The couple got to the adoption agency too late—she had already been adopted.

They were heartbroken. A year later, after Ameera's graduation, they moved to Tesano to start anew. The following year, they had Asiya.

But that was when the nightmares began. Ameera saw their faces—Hassan, Nazif, and Harissa—haunting her every night. Each day would go by with her feeling less like herself with only Harif as her anchor. His love and adoration alone kept her sane and grounded enough to continue her life with two more children and a job at the bank.

THE ATMOSPHERE GROWS HEAVY, almost solid. I replay her words in my mind and they send visceral pangs at my chest.

None of us speaks, and we remain that way until Asiya's dad enters the living room. He takes one look at us and his gait slows. His wife looks at him as if begging him to save her from something. She's crying, and not making any effort to wipe her tears.

I'm feeling so many things, feelings without names. The most dominant of all is anger. It's raging, and if I don't get out of this house, I'll say things I'll regret. I feel like I'm suffocating. I need to leave. How could anyone expect me to stay after knowing the same woman who birthed me wanted to kill me?

"What's happened?" he asks, directing the question at his wife.

She opens her mouth and closes it again. She glances at me through soaked eyes, and I look away. The feelings intensify and pull me down harder when she looks at me.

"Lila is Harissa," Asiya says. Her eyes are wet, too, but she looks pretty calm. A betting man would guess that she's happy. I'm truly her elder sister, after all. It's what we've wanted for so long a time—to be sisters bounded by blood. But under these circumstances? I couldn't be more revolted.

"Excuse me," I say, getting up.

Asiya mouths "please" at me, but I ignore her and stomp off to my room—no, the room I was given. I don't think I should call it my room anymore. There's no way I'm staying here. I don't know what I'll do when I leave, since I don't have even a penny on me, or a phone, but I really don't care. I just need to leave. I'll figure things out once I'm out of here.

"Lila," Asiya says as she barges into the room. She's breathless. "Please. Mother was young at the time. She didn't know what she was doing. And she tried to find you after she married Father, right? Please..."

"She didn't want me then. And I'm questioning if she

really wants me now, too. She tried to murder me! How do you explain that? Tell me," I say.

"I want you to stay. Please, stay."

I don't know when *she* got here, but the wind outside is louder than her voice. I don't want to care, but the agonized look on Asiya's mother's face tugs at something buried deep within me. I slump onto the bed and bury my face in my hands. I can't stop the tears now, and Asiya leaves us alone.

"I'm sorry," she says as she sits beside me. "Give me a chance to be your mother. Please." She reaches out to hold my hand, and I let her.

I'm still angry, but I feel as though every ounce of strength left my body the moment she touched me. She holds me, and even though a voice tells me to shrug her hand off, I don't. Instead, I let go of the anger, leaning into her and letting everything out through my eyes. She holds me, sobbing quietly with me.

After a while, I move away. Mami will always be my mother, but maybe it's time to allow myself to be mothered once more. I take her hands in mine and try to smile.

Asiya enters the room after Mother leaves. She looks like she had when we were over at Baba's house—brooding. She sits beside me and holds my hand, pulling it into her lap. Her lips part, and I wait for her to speak.

"Lila...Harissa, there's something I need to say to you.

Please, allow me to finish talking. I need to get it out of here." She pokes at her chest.

I nod.

"Before Debayo kidnapped me, I hated you."

My hand twitches in hers, and she holds on tighter.

"Or rather, I hated Harissa. I felt you took Mother's sanity, and by extension, you took her from us. I knew she loved us, but she spent almost all her time in her head with whatever memories she had of you. I wanted her to get better, but I didn't want you to return if you were alive. My logic was that we'd lose her forever, if you found her or she did you."

My head hurts. This is too much information for one person in a day.

"Then, I met you as Lila. You're my first real friend, you know. And believe me or not, there were moments I wished we were siblings. But even in those moments, I didn't want my elder sibling to be Harissa. Now, seeing you...knowing you, and finding out you're Harissa, I want to say I'm sorry. And I'm ashamed. I know this is hard to process. I love you. And I'm so happy you're Harissa."

She lets go of my hand and looks at me. Her eyes are teary, and she's biting her lips. The next thing I do surprises us both. I pull her into a hug. She feels stiff, like this wasn't the reaction she was expecting. After a moment, she wraps her arms around me, too. In spite of everything, I now feel I'm where I belong.

Home.

IT'S SELDOM common to be grateful for life for dealing you an ugly card, but the same cannot be said for Asiya and Lila Harissa. For the rest of their lives, each time one felt her heart tug at the other's, they'd say a silent prayer of gratitude. For all they lost and endured and received.

Ameera went months without seeing the ghosts of her past. The nightmares and episodes released their grip on her, and she had little use for Dr. Davis's pills. Her mind became quiet, and she loved her family with an apologetic intensity to make up for all the times lost. Harif felt the fullness of his wife and family; at times, he felt like the most blessed man alive.

After she made peace with her birth mother and her adoptive parents' death, Lila Harissa took on her birth name. She started university all over again, studying art.

When she entered her second year, Asiya and Assad decided to tie the knot. On the eve of the wedding, when the guests had left, and the sun was beginning to fade, the gatekeeper entered the living room and informed Lila Harissa that she had a visitor.

Everyone was perplexed, but most of all, her. Having a family and a home once more did nothing to get her out of her shell. She had moments of outspokenness, but she was still the one who'd remained quiet throughout a conversation. It was Asiya who balanced her out. She knew just how to get her sister to talk and be excited about something.

Lila Harissa had no love interest at twenty-eight, and it was a relief that nobody talked about her non-existent love life. She was focused on her education and family, and everyone in the family was staunchly supportive of her. So, it was of no surprise that she remained seated, eyebrows raised and a confused expression on her face. It took Ameera's reminder that it was rude to keep a visitor waiting to move her out of the couch on which she was sitting.

She followed the gatekeeper to the gate. Lila Harissa stopped in her tracks when she saw her visitor's back— she'd recognize that back anywhere. He spun around, the pain and hope in his eyes staring back at her.

Zayn looked the same as he appeared in her imagination and, occasionally, in her dreams.

"Am I too late?" he asked. He walked towards her to where she stood rooted in the spot, maintaining a considerable distance between them.

She stared, trying to find her words.

"I know I shouldn't have run off like that, and I have no business showing up here after so long. I was just scared... about you...if you...if you felt...I didn't want you to think I'd taken advantage of your situation." He stood there for what felt like eons, and when she still didn't say anything—only looked at him with a look bordering on disbelief and hurt and love—he spoke again, this time with his shoulders slightly hunched in defeat. "I get that this is weird. I'll leave right away if you want me to."

He turned on his heels, but before he could take a step, she remembered one word: "Stay."

She heard someone clear their throat behind her and whisked around to find both Asiya and Assad grinning.

"I suppose we'll have another wedding soon," Asiya said, winking. Lila Harissa rolled her eyes, and Zayn broke out into a smile. "In Shaa Allah."

END

My first thanks to the One who never slumbers, who is always with me and keeps me anchored.

I want to thank myself for believing in me and never giving up. To the Shaherazad Shelves team, thank you for loving my story and helping to bring my book into the world.

Thanks to my closest friend and confidant who has been a support for me throughout this journey. To Adnan, Hummu, Bilkis, Mimi, George; thank you for all you do.

Kataru Yahya is a Ghanaian writer, poet, and medical sonographer. Her interest in writing started when she was only fourteen, and she hopes to contribute to the proper representation of Muslims in literature. Kataru's poetry has been featured in the literary magazine Ta Adesa and Writer's Space Africa — Ghana. Outside of writing, she loves to read or rewatch her favorite shows.

HOME IS A SILHOUETTE is her debut novel. You can find her on social media using @kforkataru.

9 781960 323002